The Japanese Yokai Handbook

A Guide to the Spookiest Ghosts, Demons, Monsters and Evil Creatures from Japanese Folklore

Masami Kinoshita

TUTTLE Publishing

Tokyo | Rutland, Vermont | Singapore

Contents

Why I Wrote this Book 6
What Is a Yokai? 8

Chapter 1: Super Scary Yokai
Ippon Datara 16
Kowai (Scary) 18
Shunobon 20
Kiyohime 22
Kasha (Fire Cart) 23
Gagoze 24
Nozuji 25
Nekomata 26
Hainu (Winged Dog) 27
Yamamba 28
Satori 29
Tomokazuki 30
Kunekune 31
Koromo-dako (Robe Octopus) 32
Ningyo (Mermaid) 33
Question 1: Yokai Questions 34

Chapter 2: Super Mysterious Yokai
Uwan 38
Asaoke no Ke (Asaoke Hair) 40
Nakanekozou (Nakane Brat) 42
Azukiarai (Red Bean Washer) 44
Yagyou-San (Mr. Nightwalker) 45
Kudan 46
Hitokusai (I-Smell-Human) 47
Chin Chin Kobakama 48
Otoroshi 49
Shiri-Haguri 50

Sennenmogura (Thousand-Year-Old Mole) 51
Kashambo 52
Makuragaeshi (Pillow Swapper) 53
Chinchirori 54
Peroritaro (Licky Boy) 55
Nurarihyon 56
Karasu Ojisan (Uncle Crow) 57
Zashikiwarashi 58
Aburasumashi 59
Case 1: Yokai Report 60

Chapter 3: Super Powerful Yokai

Yamata no Orochi 64
Ushioni (Ox Demon) 66
Akaragashira 68
Kincho-Tanuki 69
Shutendoji 70
Tsuchigumo 71
Tamamonomae 72
Tengu 73
Case 2: Yokai Report 74

Chapter 4: Super Weird Yokai

Tenaga-Ashinaga (Long-Limbed Giants) 78
Tenome (Eye Hands) 80
Kainade 82
Nuppepo 83
Otekurebaba (Piggy-Back-Ride-Me Granny) 84
Keukegen 85
Nandobaba (Storage Room Granny) 86
Chirami Kozo (Lurking Brat) 87
Question 2: Yokai Questions 88
Question 3: Yokai Questions 89

🔥 Chapter 5: Super Cute Yokai

Betobetosan (Mr. Sticky) 92
Kusabira 94
Notabozu 96
Sunekosuri 97
Sodehikikozou (Sleeve Tugging Brat) 98
Kijimuna 99
Question 4: Yokai Questions 100

🔥 Chapter 6: Super Simple Yokai

Sumitsuke (Painter) 104
Nurikabe (Painted Wall) 105
Akakgo (Baby) 106
Ao Nyobo (Blue Lady) 107
Oshiroi-Baba (Powder Granny) 108
Yanari 109
Yosuzume (Night Sparrow) 110
Enenra 111
Hohonade (Cheek Rubber) 112
Kamaitachi 113
Question 5: Yokai Questions 114

🔥 Chapter 7: Super Sad Yokai

Nue 118
Ganborinyudo 120
Janjanbi 122
Okikumushi 123
Mokurikokuri 124
Tatarimokke 125
Iwanabouzu 126
Soroban Bozu (Abacus Boy) 127
Ubume 128
San no Maru-Gaeru (Castle Outskirt Frogs) 129
Case 3: Yokai Report 130

Chapter 8: Super Kind Yokai

Hakutaku 134
Kamikiri (Haircutter) 136
Akaname (Grime Licker) 138
Senpoku Kanpoku 139
Shizuka Mochi (Quiet Mochi) 140
Okuri Ookami (Watcher Wolf) 141
Kanedama 142
Baku 143
Question 6: Yokai Questions 144

Chapter 9: Super Evil Yokai

Kanibouzu (Crab Monk) 148
Daru 150
Pauchi Kamui 151
Hamaguri Nyobo (Clam Wife) 152
Nikusui 153
Bimbogami (Poor God) 154
Shinguri Makuri 155
Case 4: Yokai Report 156

Chapter 10: Super Stupid Yokai

Biro-N 160
Tantankororin 162
Dorotabo 163
Nebutori 164
Usuoibaba 165
Tsukehimokozo 166
Tofukozo (Tofu Boy) 167
Okkeruipe 168
Kappa 169
Case 5: Yokai Report 171

Yokai List 172
Final Words 174

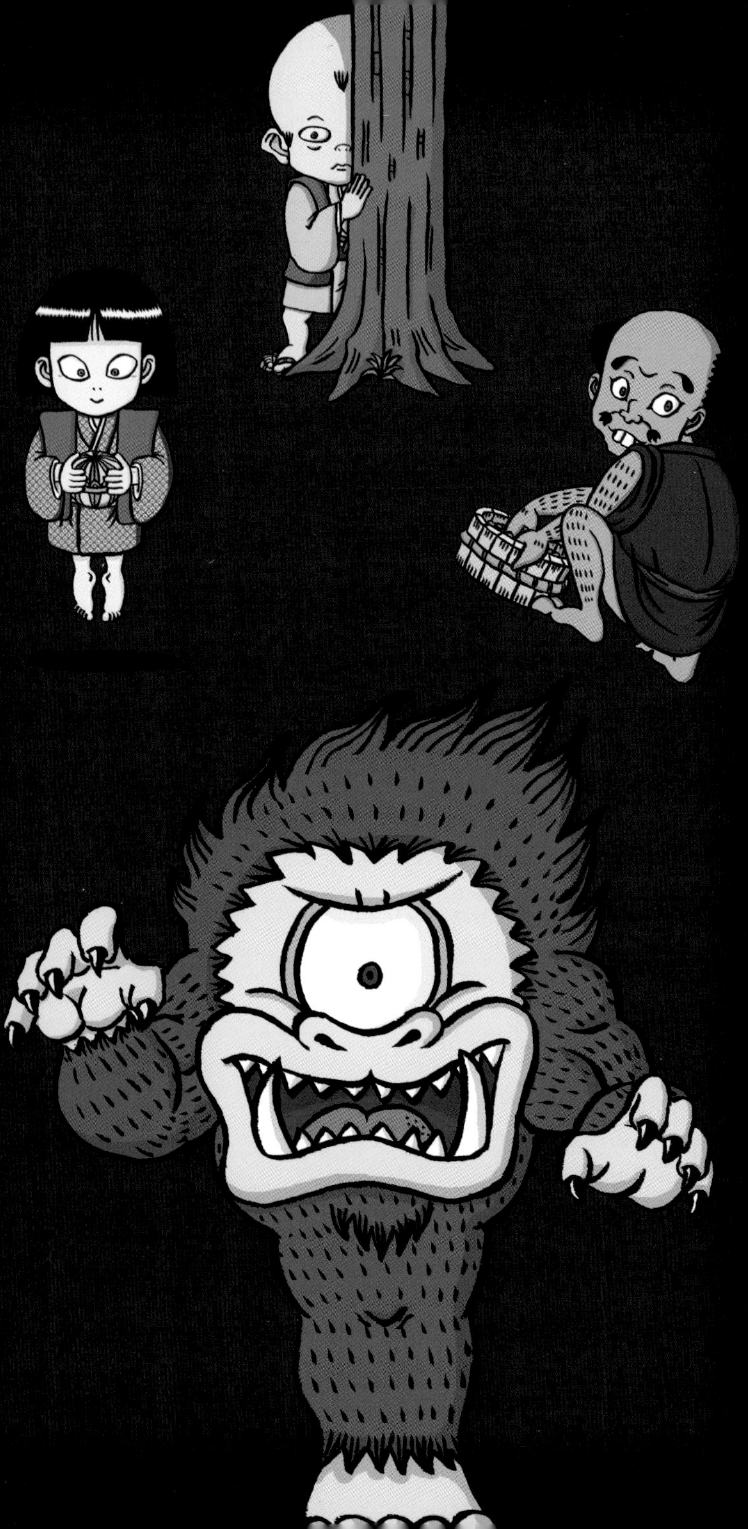

Why I Wrote this Book

The world is filled with mysterious things, beings that usually can't be seen with the naked eye. These creatures are sometimes called demons, sometimes ghosts and sometimes monsters.

Over the years, as we learned more about them, we identified each of these odd entity's identities. We now call these beings "Yokai" and there are many kinds out there, from scary Yokai to cute Yokai, sad Yokai and even Yokai that are a little stupid.

Just like humans, each Yokai has its own style. In this book, I wanted to show the wide variety of these fascinating creatures. So I will be introducing Yokai by grouping them into easily identifiable categories. Of course, even within these categories, each Yokai can have unique powers, personalities and purpose. This is a perfect opportunity to learn about all of the Yokai you've never heard of before.

Now, are you ready to meet some Yokai?

—Masami Kinoshita

Hyakki Yagyo by Kawanabe Kyosai

What Is a Yokai?

Is it a monster?

Is it a demon?

Are they different from each other?

The famous Japanese writer Kunio Yanagita once said that when a god falls, it becomes a Yokai. However, after many people have studied Yokai, it seems that the way we perceive them is now changing. Still, we have not developed a clear answer to the question of what a Yokai really is. Yokai can be demons, ghosts, goblins and many other kinds of supernatural beings. A Yokai is a creature that can be defined in many different ways.

An important aspect of Yokai is their connection to the land. Although we don't know everything about them, we've had reports of many Yokai sightings over the years. This information, in the case of Japanese Yokai, can help write the history of the human culture of the region in which the Yokai appears. You might say that Yokai are a tool for us to learn about ourselves.

Are Yokai always scary?

Have you ever heard someone say, "If you do something bad, a ghost will get you!" This is a clever way of using the power of Yokai to stop kids from acting up.

Some Yokai are terrifying, while others bring happiness. It is important to know that not all Yokai are bad or scary.

This book introduces the various kinds of Yokai have, not only the scary ones, but also the stupid ones and the cute ones. You may be frightened by the terrifying stories, or you may laugh at their stupidity. By the time you finish this book, I am sure you will be able to see Yokai with a new perspective.

Where do Yokai live?

"There are a lot of stories about Yokai in Osaka, aren't there?"

"I heard that there were many Yokai in Tokyo, is it true?"

"There are quite a few Yokai seen in Kyoto, right?"

The name of the Yokai, Kowai (page 18) is a play on the Japanese word 'kowai' which means scary.

I get a lot of questions like these about where Yokai appear. My answers to these questions are both "yes" and "no." Here's why...

Let's say a mysterious creature appears out of nowhere. Nobody knows what it is or where it came from. But since everyone in that place all experienced it, they try to pass on the story to future generations. Over the years, as the stories become legends, the Yokai start to take form. They are clearly connected to a certain place and become important to its people.

Yokai have appeared in ancient scrolls and prints, in folk tales and gossip, in newspapers, radio, and television, and in stories that people have told and retold. Wherever there are people, there are Yokai. In other words, Yokai live on in the history of the people who experience them.

When did Yokai first appear?

Tales of monsters have been around for many, many years but the term "Yokai" has not been used for all that long. In the year 797, during the early Heian period of Japan, the book *Shoku-nihongi* describes an exorcism performed because of the presence of a being called a "Yokai." This is the earliest use of the term, however, it did not take root at the time.

It wasn't until the Meiji period (1868–1912) that the word "Yokai" came back into the spotlight. The word became established as a term used by researchers and historians. From that point on, it became a popular word to describe these supernatural beings.

While it is impossible to know exactly when these legends began to be passed down, I like to say that the moment people told their stories is when Yokai were born.

Yamata no Orochi (page 64) is a serpent youkai that appears in history books such as *Kojiki* and *Nihon Shoki*.

Are there Yokai around today?

As you read this book and learn about Yokai like the Rokurokubi or Nopperabo you may wonder, "Why don't I hear any stories about them now?" The easiest answer is, these are not the ony kind of Yokai. I believe that wherever there are people, there are always Yokai and that Yokai will live on as long as human beings exist.

As time passes, new Yokai will continue to be born. For example, there are Yokai that were born on the Internet. Because we live in a modern society where the Internet is widespread, it's natural that Yokai would be a part of that world, even if its a virtual one.

As long as we are interested and aware of their existence, Yokai will never disappear from our lives.

Kunekune (page 31) is a 21st century Yokai that first appeared on the Internet.

Chapter 1

Super Scary Yokai

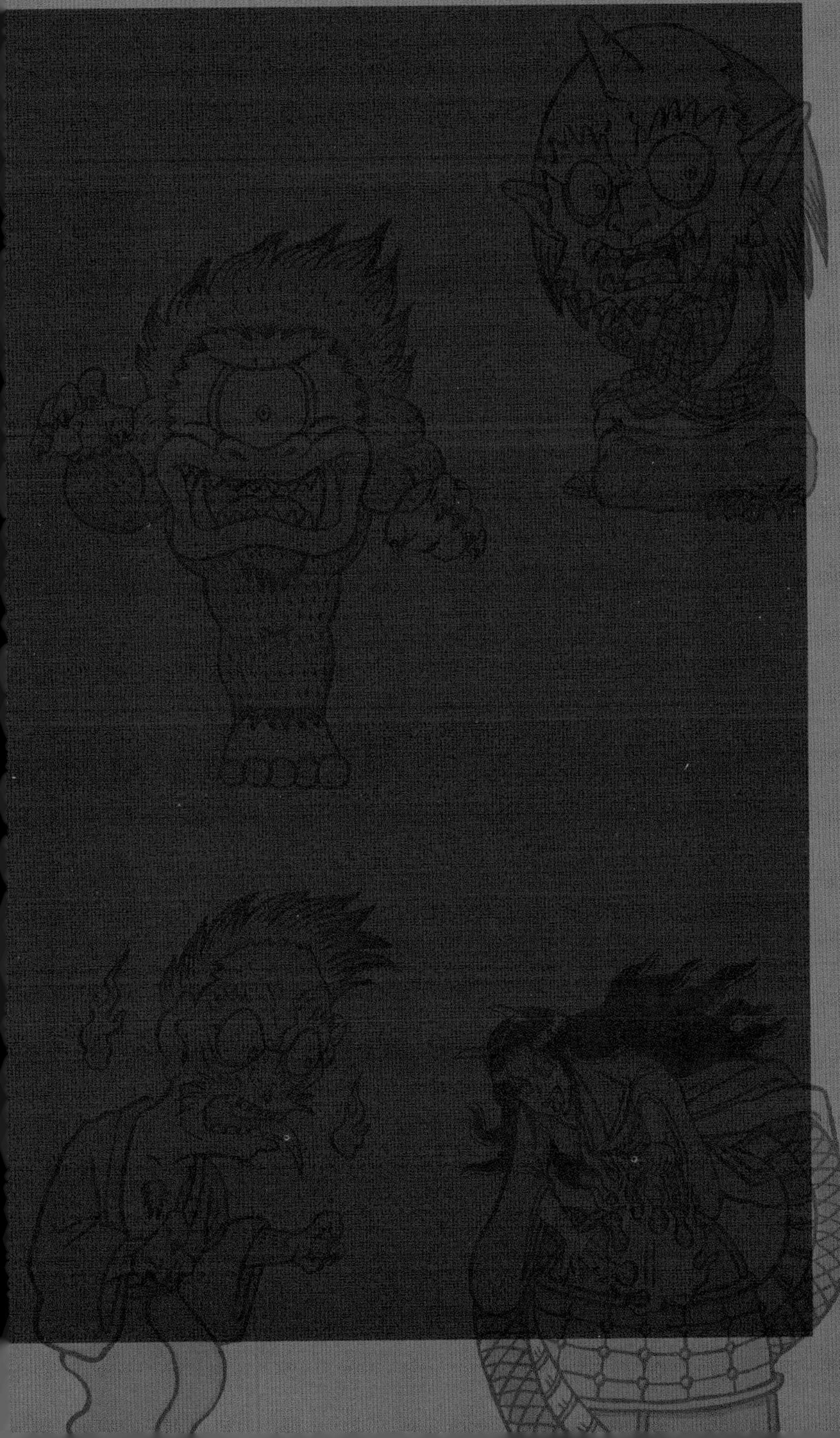

Ippon Datara

A one legged monster who attacks only humans in the mountains on December 20th.

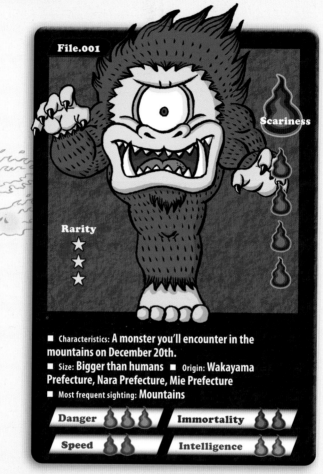

File.001

Scariness

Rarity
★
★
★

- Characteristics: A monster you'll encounter in the mountains on December 20th.
- Size: Bigger than humans ■ Origin: Wakayama Prefecture, Nara Prefecture, Mie Prefecture
- Most frequent sighting: Mountains

Danger	Immortality
Speed	Intelligence

Ippon Datara will appear from the mountains on December 20th. Usually it means no harm, but it is said that on December 20th, Ippon Datara will have no mercy on humans who try to hike through the mountains.

It may be known as a one legged spirit but depending on the region, it also appears as a cyclops. It often frequents the border between Nara and Wakayama prefectures, as well as the mountains of Kii Peninsula.

When you visit areas where Ippon Datara resides, you'll also find stories of other one legged spirits. Also, the Datara part of its name is also related to the word "Tatara setetsu," which is a bellow operated with one leg.

This is SUPER Scary!

▶ There are many scary stories told by people who go into the mountains on December 20th.

▶ It is said that this Yokai has one eye that is as big as a dinner plate.

▶ It moves around by hopping on one leg. It is said that it can even do somersaults with it.

Interesting Fact

Since it has one leg and one eye, It might be related to the Tatara Setetsu (one leg bellow). It must be a hard life to live with one leg/one eye.

Kowai (Scary)

Glaring at food with bloodshotted eyes?! A gluttonous spirit.

File.002

Rarity ★ ★

Scariness

MAX!

- Characteristics: **Even after death it is obsessed with food, so much that it'll scavenge for anything it can eat.**
- Size: **About the same as a human**
- Origin: **Unknown**
- Most frequent sighting: **Towns**

Danger	Immortality
Speed	Intelligence

When a gluttenous being is unable to attain Buddhahood after death, its delusional thoughts take on the form of Kowai. It is said that Kowai will attempt to hinder others from entering the Buddhahood afterlife.

In the Edo period (1603–1867), the character for Kowai in the book *One Hundred Stories of Picture Books* was written using characters for Fox 狐(ko) Person 者(wa) Odd 異(i). In Japanese, "kowai" means "scary." Legends say that when we describe something as scary in Japanese, the word came from this Yokai. Kowai is described as having a bent back, sharp fangs, three fingers, and no legs. If you look at it closely, you'll see its eyes are bloodshot as it tries to eat some udon noodles. Its obsession with food is very SCARY.

This is SUPER Scary!

🔥 A wandering spirit that couldn't rest in peace.

🔥 It may be dead but it scavenges for food without no real purpose.

▶ It glares at food with all its might.

▶ Its long pointy tongue hangs out.

Interesting Fact

It may change its appearance based on where and when you see it. It is said that Kowai has countless forms.

Shunobon

A Yokai with a face so horrifying, it'll literally scare you to death!

File.003

Rarity
★
★

Scariness

MAX!

- Characteristics: **Its power is to simply scare people to death.**
- Size: **About the same as a person**
- Origin: **Fukushima and Nigata Prefectures**
- Most frequent sighting: **Streets at night**

| Danger | | | | Immortality | | | |
| Speed | | | | Intelligence | | | |

Shunobon is a terrifying ghost whose lore has been handed down mainly in Fukushima and Nigata prefectures. According to the Edo period book *An Old Woman's Tale*, Shunobon has a bright red face, eyes the size of plates, hair like needles, a large horn that grows from its forehead and a mouth that opens up to its ears. The sound of its teeth clattering is said to be as loud and furious as thunderclaps.

Legend has it that one day many years ago, a Samurai came across Shunobon and was so terrified that he fled to a nearby house where he was let in by a lady. Unfortunately for him, the lady also turned into a monster. The poor Samurai was so terrified that he dropped dead on the spot.

This is Super Scary!

First and foremost, Shunobon is incredibly frightening.

▶ Its face is red and it has a large horn growing from its forehead.

▶ The sound it makes when it clenches its jaws is like thunder.

▶ It has nasty fangs as sharp as needles.

Interesting Fact

Shunobon is a Yokai that is so horrifying it will frighten you to your core.

Kiyohime

Love turned to anger, it has a terrifying snake form.

File.004

Scariness

Rarity
★★

- Characteristics: **She's had it with cowardly men who are filled with lies so she has taken a snake form.**
- Size: **Over 33 ft. (10 m)** ▪ Origin: **Ki Province**
- Most frequent sighting: **Dojoji Temple**

Danger	Immortality
Speed	Intelligence

Kiyohime was originally a woman who became a snake out of her love for a man. This story has been passed down through the ages, including the Heian book called *Hokke Genki*.

In the story, a monk named Anchin pays a visit to Kumano. Kiyohime falls in love with Anchin at first sight and aggressively attacks him, but she gets tired of Anchin's attempt to avoid her. Kiyohime finally gets so angry with Anchin that she chases after him in the form of a snake. It is said that Kiyohime took her own life after burning Anchin who escaped to Dojoji Temple.

The sad story of Anchin and Kiyohime has been depicted in Japanese theater, Ningyo Joruri (puppet drama), and Kabuki, and has been handed down to the present day.

Kasha (Fire Cart)

A Yokai that appears at funerals to rob the corpse. It turns out its true form is a cat!

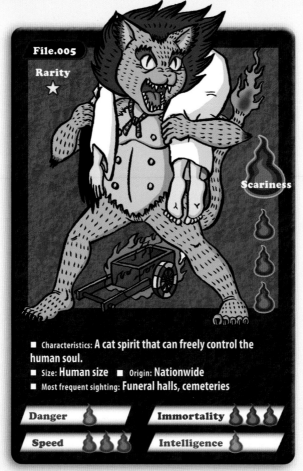

File.005

Rarity
★

Scariness

- ■ Characteristics: **A cat spirit that can freely control the human soul.**
- ■ Size: **Human size** ■ Origin: **Nationwide**
- ■ Most frequent sighting: **Funeral halls, cemeteries**

Danger		Immortality	
Speed		Intelligence	

Kasha is a Yokai that robs corpses away from funerals and gravesites. But in some areas its true identity is assumed to be a cat. The story of missing corpses and Kasha have been widely passed down throughout the country.

Even today, people say that when a cat straddles a coffin, the dead come back to life. It seems that Kasha can also put a soul into the corpse. It's been said that if the dead start moving, you should hit it with a broomstick.

Kasha is also said to have the power to hang the souls of people who have done wrong from pine trees, and may also have the power to manipulate people's souls at will.

Gagoze

It appears out of nowhere attacking people late at night.

File.006

Scariness

MAX!

Rarity
★

- Characteristics: **A Yokai that appears around Gangoji Temple.**
- Size: **Around the size of a human**
- Origin: **Nara Prefecture** ■Most frequent place: **Gangoji Temple**

Danger				Immortality	

Speed			Intelligence		

Gagoze appears out of nowhere and will attack and kill people at night. They are said to have appeared at Genkoji Temple in Nara during the Asuka Period. It also appeared in *Nihon ryoiki*, Japan's oldest collection of Buddhist tales. In an Edo period book titled *Gazu Hyakki Yagyo*, Gagoze is depicted wearing a cloth-like object and looking almost like a person.

According to the story, Gagoze was exterminated by the son of thunder, probably because he was a terrifying being. The phrase "Gagoze will come for you (if you do bad things)" is still used in many places. Depending on the region, it is also called Gangoze.

Nozuji

A Yokai with no legs, no hands, no nose, and no eyes, just a mouth to bite people.

File.007

Rarity ★★★

Scariness

- Characteristics: It looks a little like a hammer and usually feeds on rabbits.
- Size: Approximately 12–35 in. (30–90 cm)
- Origin: Around Kinki and Hokuriku
- Most frequent place: Mountains

Danger		Immortality	
Speed		Intelligence	

Noziji is a ghost shaped like a mallet, of which stories are heard in many places. It is sometimes confused with the aardvark. It lives in the mountains and eats rabbits and other animals. When it sees people, it rolls over and bites them on the leg. It seems to be an unusual looking creature with no eyes or nose.

It is recorded in the Edo-period books *Shinano Kisho Roku* and *Wakan Sansai Zue* that it is 12 in. (30.2 cm) in length and 12 in. (30 cm) in thickness, and its body length and diameter are approximately 3 ft. (90 cm) and 6 in. (15 cm), respectively.

Nekomata

Once a pet, now a wandering cat spirit living in the mountains.

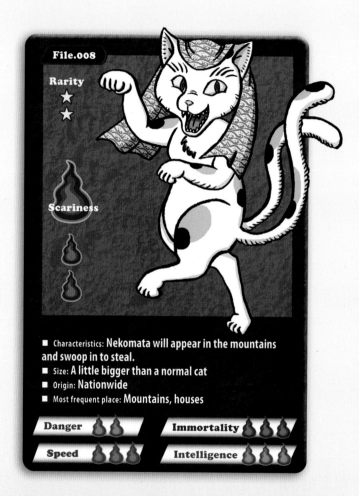

File.008

Rarity ★ ★

Scariness

- Characteristics: Nekomata will appear in the mountains and swoop in to steal.
- Size: A little bigger than a normal cat
- Origin: Nationwide
- Most frequent place: Mountains, houses

Danger	Immortality
Speed	Intelligence

Some people believe that the Nekomata is the result of a cat that has turned into a monster. Some of them taunt or attack people. The oldest record of Nekomata in Japan so far is from a book called *Meigetsu-ki* from the Kamakura period (1185–1333). The Nekomata in this book are very ferocious. Its body is very large, and there are records of it devouring and killing humans. It is said to have appeared in what is now Nara Prefecture, but it may be a slightly different species from the cats we know today.

Since cats have been a part of people's lives since ancient times, many strange stories have been told about them.

Hainu (Winged Dog)

A dog spirit with wings and strong fighting ability. It'll attack humans and feed on livestock

File.009

Rarity
★
★

Scariness

- Characteristics: It's so strong as if it was trained to fight in a war.
- Size: About the same as a regular dog
- Origin: All around Fukuoka Prefecture
- Most frequent place: Unknown

Danger

Immortality

Speed

Intelligence

It is said that the Hainu was a ferocious thing, attacking people and devouring livestock. Some say that it was a dog that the great Samurai Toyotomi Hideyoshi adored, while others say that its power prevented Hideyoshi from carrying out his plans. Whether Hainu was a foe or a friend of Hideyoshi, we're still unsure. But in any case, it is said to have been a mysterious dog with wings.

The story of Hainu is told in Chikugo City, Fukuoka Prefecture. There's even a place called Hainuzuka in the area. There, you'll find a temple called Zougaku which has been said to have been built as a memorial to the winged dog, Hainu.

Yamamba

A female Yokai that'll visit a village from the mountains and feed on humans.

File.010

Rarity

★
★

Scariness

- ■ Characteristics: **A Yokai that'll wander into human villages from the mountains and terrorize humans.**
- ■ Size: **About the same as humans**
- ■ Origin: **Nationwide**
- ■ Most frequent place: **Mountains, small villages**

Danger	Immortality
Speed	Intelligence

Yamamba is a female ghost that haunts the mountains. Stories of Yamamba have been told in many places throughout Japan. She has long hair, a slit mouth, and a frightening face that looks as if she might take a person and eat them. In folk tales, too, there is a horrifying Yamamba who takes people and eats them.

On the other hand, there are also Yamamba that do not harm people, those that bestow good fortune, and those that are worshiped as gods. That is how familiar Yamamba must be to people's hearts.

Satori

A Yokai that'll appear out of nowhere in the mountains and read your mind.

File.011

Rarity
★
★
★

Scariness

- ■ Characteristics: **It can understand human languages and will read your mind.**
- ■ Size: **About the same as humans**
- ■ Origin: **Nationwide**
- ■ Most frequent place: **Mountains**

Danger

Immortality

Speed

Intelligence

Satori is a ghost that can read people's thoughts and haunts the mountains.

The hairy Satori appears in an Edo-period book titled *Konjaku Gazu Zoku Hyakki*. According to the book, Satori can read people's minds, but will not harm them. Even if a frightened person plans to kill him or her, Satori reads his or her mind and simply runs away before he or she can do any harm.

In other stories, Satori is turned into a Yokai that kills people and sucks their blood. But even in that case, it was chased away by people throwing firewood at it. At the end of the day, Satori is a Yokai that runs away.

Tomokazuki

Once you dive into the ocean this Yokai will mirror your appearance.

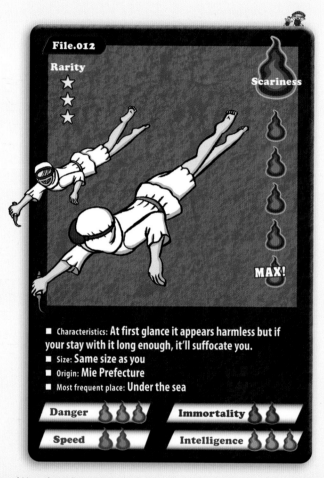

- ■ Characteristics: **At first glance it appears harmless but if your stay with it long enough, it'll suffocate you.**
- ■ Size: **Same size as you**
- ■ Origin: **Mie Prefecture**
- ■ Most frequent place: **Under the sea**

Danger 🍶🍶🍶   **Immortality** 🍶🍶

Speed 🍶🍶   **Intelligence** 🍶🍶🍶

Tomokazuki is a ghost that appears in the sea. It seems to be disguised as a person who dives in the sea to deceive people.

The story is often told in Mie Prefecture. In Japanese, Tomokazuki is written as "共潜き" meaning "dive together." A story has been handed down by Ama, female divers who collect shells and seaweed. Once the Ama dove into the ocean and suddenly encountered a person who looked exactly like her. She said, if the look-alike kindly offers you abalone, do not accept it. It is said that if you follow them, it may lead you to drowning to death.

Divers who are afraid of meeting a Tomokazuki protect themselves by attaching a grid and star-shaped mark called a "Doman-Seman" to their clothing and tools.

Kunekune

A Yokai that looks like an enormous octopus. It can expand its body and consume ships at sea.

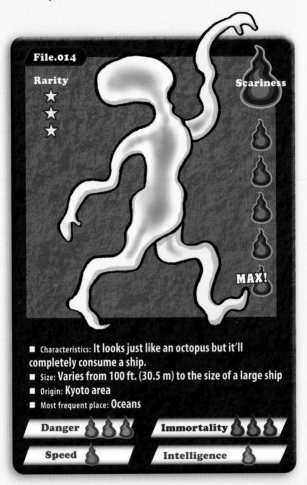

File.014

Rarity
★
★
★

Scariness

MAX!

- ■ Characteristics: It looks just like an octopus but it'll completely consume a ship.
- ■ Size: Varies from 100 ft. (30.5 m) to the size of a large ship
- ■ Origin: Kyoto area
- ■ Most frequent place: Oceans

Danger

Immortality

Speed

Intelligence

The Kunekune is a relatively new ghost that has been heard about mainly on Internet forums since the beginning of the 21st century. It is said to cause psychosis when seen, and as its name suggests, it is a wiggling ghost.

The story told on the Internet is that in the countryside, one of the brothers saw something that is said to be forbidden to be seen, and he starts losing his mind. The stories of Kunekune is gradually evolving.

Koromo-dako (Robe Octopus)

A Yokai that looks like an enormous octopus. It'll expand its body so big and consume the ship.

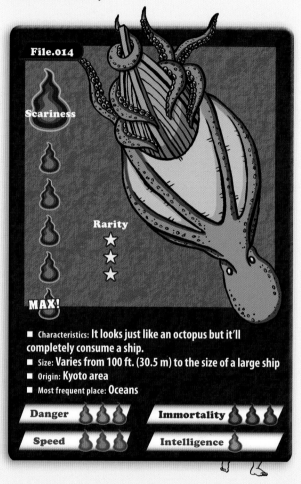

File.014

Scariness

Rarity
★
★
★

MAX!

- Characteristics: **It looks just like an octopus but it'll completely consume a ship.**
- Size: **Varies from 100 ft. (30.5 m) to the size of a large ship**
- Origin: **Kyoto area**
- Most frequent place: **Oceans**

| Danger | Immortality |
| Speed | Intelligence |

The Koromo-dako is a ghost of the sea and looks no different from an ordinary octopus.

However, it is said that it is so huge that it spreads its body like a robe, swallowing people and boats alike, and submerging them in the sea.

The story is passed down to Yosa County in Kyoto Prefecture. In some areas, the actual purple octopuses are called Koromo-dako.

The purple octopus is quite large when its tentacles are spread out. But even so, it's not large to the point that it can envelop a boat or a person. But I guess the octopus looks like a ghost as it spits ink from its boneless body. At this point, you might not even be able to tell if you encountered a ghost or just a very big octopus.

Ningyo (Mermaid)

Part human, part fish—the mysterious creature that resides in the sea.

- Characteristics: **They're sometimes eaten by humans and sometimes they retaliate.**
- Size: **Around the same size as a human**
- Origin: **All around the world**
- Most frequent place: **Oceans & rivers**

Ningyo make the sea their home, like mermaids. There are many stories about mermaids that have been handed down. The oldest record of what appears to be a Ningyo in Japan is found in *Nihongi*, a book from the Nara period (710–794).

It is said to have appeared in areas around present-day Shiga and Osaka prefectures. Ningyo is said to have been neither a fish nor a person, although it looked like a child.

Although the word Ningyo was not used to describe these mysterious beings at the time, we know that they were half man and half fish. Legends say that anyone who harms a Ningyo will receive some form of retribution, but there is also a story that If you eat mermaid meat, it will bring longevity.

Yokai Questions

Question
1

What should I do if I want to see Yokai?

If you want to see a Yokai, you'll have to go where Yokai are rumored to be seen.

First, you'll have to learn about the Yokai you want to meet. Gathering information is the most important step. Read a lot of books to research about the Yokai. Explore books of different genres. Try picking a fairytale or a book of fables and you'll be surprised with the information you can find. From there you might get some hints on where and when the Yokai you want to meet.

usually appears. The more research you do, surely, the more you want to meet that Yokai. When you're ready, be sure to consult an adult before you try visiting the actual location and you might encounter something.

If you are unable to meet the Yokai, you may find something unexpected by talking directly to people who live in the area where Yokai are said to appear. It may be best if you try talking to those who have been around the temple or shrines for a very long time.

Chapter 2

Super Mysterious Yokai

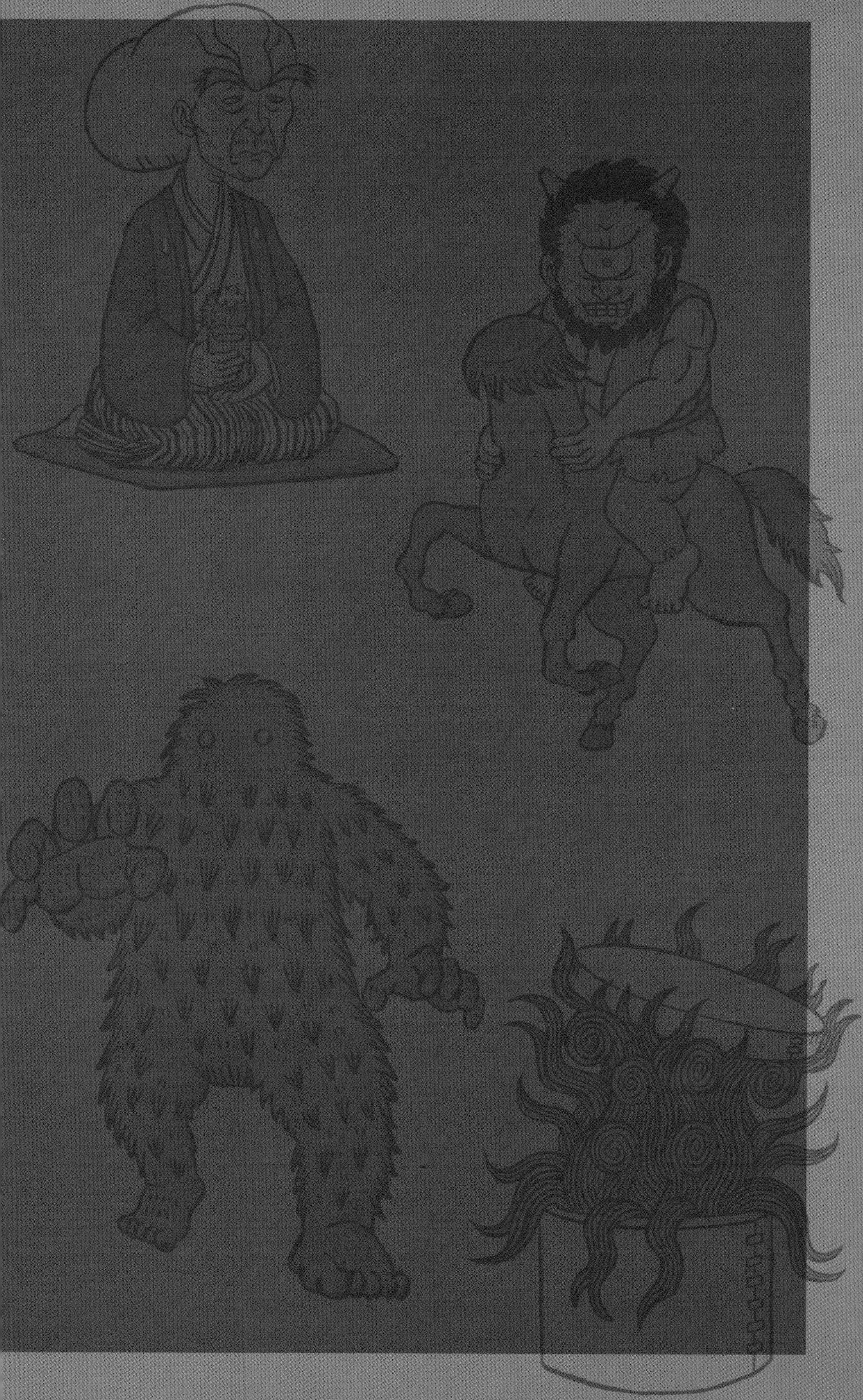

Uwan

A tuft of hair that was kept and used to connect with God.

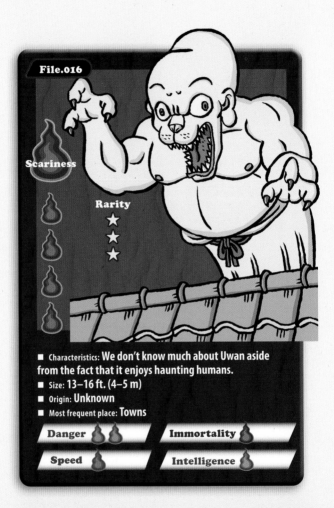

File.016

Scariness

Rarity
★
★
★

- Characteristics: We don't know much about Uwan aside from the fact that it enjoys haunting humans.
- Size: 13–16 ft. (4–5 m)
- Origin: Unknown
- Most frequent place: Towns

Danger	Immortality
Speed	Intelligence

Uwan is a powerful ghost that appears in the Edo period picture scrolls "Hyakkai Zukan" and "Gazu Hyakki Yagyo," but we do not know exactly what kind of ghost it is because there is no description in the picture scrolls.

The "Hyakkai Zukan" picture shows Uwan as a black creature with black teeth, three fingers, and with its arms up in a threatening gesture. Meanwhile in "Gazu Hyakki Yagyo," Uwan appears leaning out from the wall of a building. Perhaps it is a large ghost? One thing that both versions of Uwan share is that it always seems to be looking down, but what is he looking at? Maybe he is looking for something important. No one knows for sure.

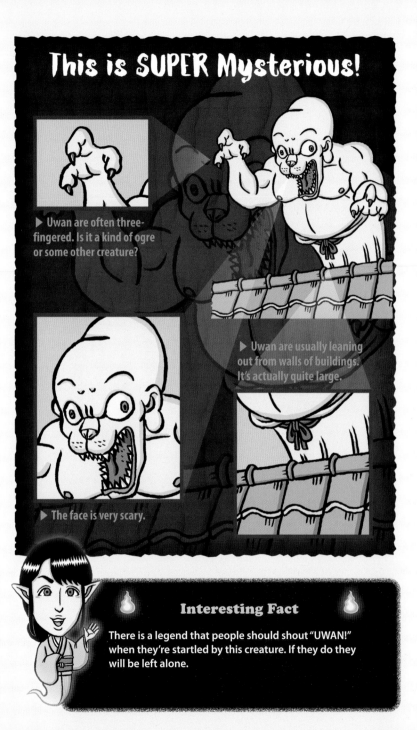

This is SUPER Mysterious!

▶ Uwan are often three-fingered. Is it a kind of ogre or some other creature?

▶ Uwan are usually leaning out from walls of buildings. It's actually quite large.

▶ The face is very scary.

Interesting Fact

There is a legend that people should shout "UWAN!" when they're startled by this creature. If they do they will be left alone.

Asaoke no Ke (Asaoke Hair)

A strand of hair that was kept and used to connect with God.

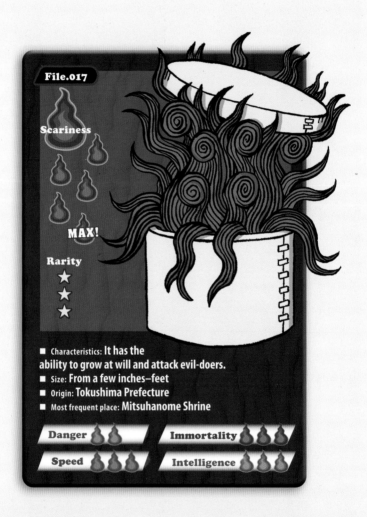

File.017

Scariness

MAX!

Rarity
★
★
★

- Characteristics: **It has the ability to grow at will and attack evil-doers.**
- Size: **From a few inches–feet**
- Origin: **Tokushima Prefecture**
- Most frequent place: **Mitsuhanome Shrine**

Danger 🍐🍐

Immortality 🍐🍐🍐

Speed 🍐🍐🍐

Intelligence 🍐🍐🍐

As the name implies, Asoke no-Ke is a mysterious hairball that was placed inside the shrine's asaoke, a kind of hemp basket. The story is told in Kamo Village, Miyoshi County, Tokushima Prefecture.

At a shrine called Mitsuhanome Shrine, a string of hairs placed in an asaoke shows its power to communicate with God by growing larger at will. It even has the ability to attack people who perform deeds. It's a mystery where these hairs came from.

This is SUPER Mysterious!

▶ Usually it's just a ball of hair.

▶ At shrines, it is usually filled with hemp threads

▶ It can grow longer and attack bad people

Interesting Fact

It is not uncommon for hair to be worshipped as part of the body of a deity. It is a bit strange to think about the fact that the hair grows when it gets angry.

Nakanekozou (Nakane Brat)

A giant hairy monster sealed away at the peak of a mountain.

File.018

Scariness

Rarity
★
★
★

- Characteristics: **A giant monster that grows hair all over its body... and face!**
- Size: **So large it can almost touch the clouds**
- Origin: **Shimokitayama Village in Nara Prefecture**
- Most frequent place: **Nagane Pass**

Danger

Immortality

Speed

Intelligence

It is said that Nakane's name may refer to Nakane Pass in Shimokitayama Village, Nara Prefecture. It seems to be a monster that appears around that area.

It has two arms and two legs, and looks like a person, but it has hair all over its face. It's far from being a "little boy" so why do people refer to it as a "brat?" The Nakanekozou harms people, so the monks have locked it up at the top of the mountain pass.

Villagers who feared this ghost used to hold a festival on the 24th day of the Lunar New Year. Currently, that is no longer done.

This is SUPER Mysterious!

▶ Its shape looks similar to humans

▶ Hair grows all over its face

▶ It is said that it grows tall enough to touch the clouds

Interesting Fact

They are described as looking like large mountain men. Most mountain men are said to be large, hairy, half-naked men.

Azukiarai (Red Bean Washer)

A Yokai that makes noise while washing red beans by the riverbank or sometimes by a lake.

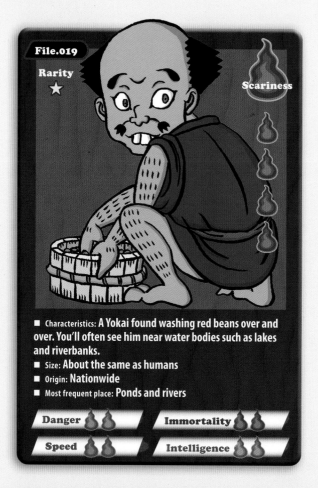

File.019

Rarity
★

Scariness

■ Characteristics: **A Yokai found washing red beans over and over. You'll often see him near water bodies such as lakes and riverbanks.**
■ Size: **About the same as humans**
■ Origin: **Nationwide**
■ Most frequent place: **Ponds and rivers**

Danger

Immortality

Speed

Intelligence

Azukiarai is a Yokai that can't be seen, but you can hear the very unique sound it makes when it's washing red beans by the river. Although you hear stories about Azukiarai all over Japan, we still don't know much about it.

In the book *Ehon Hyaku Monogatari* from the Edo period, Azukiarai makes an appearance. You can tell it's the sound that Azukiarai makes because you can hear the "shwa shwa" sound that is similar to the one made when you wash rice before cooking it. It's a Yokai that has been known for a very long time. It often appears near riverbanks, ponds, or any waterbody. We have no idea why it's constantly washing beans.

Yagyou-San (Mr. Nightwalker)

A ghost that'll appear regularly wanders around the night on a headless horse.

File.020

Rarity
★
★

Scariness

- ■ Characteristics: **It'll often appear on the night of unlucky days, New Year's Eve and Setsubun.**
- ■ Size: **About the same as humans**
- ■ Origin: **Tokushima Prefecture**
- ■ Most frequent place: **Roads at night**

| Danger | | | | Immortality | | | |
| Speed | | | | Intelligence | | |

Yagyou-San appears on fixed days, such as the day of abomination known as Yagyohi, New Year's Eve, Setsubun, and Koshin. On these days, Yagyou-San is said to roam around on a decapitated horse.

This Yagyou-San and the headless horse, however, they are not two in one, and the headless horse alone is sometimes referred to as Yagyou-San. If you meet them with this headless horse, you may be thrown or kicked to death, so be careful. There is also a story about a man who puts his sandals on his head which made Yagyou-San plop down to the ground and save the man's life. So if you encounter Yagyou-San, why don't you give it a try?

Kudan

Death right after birth?! It often foretells ominous fortune…

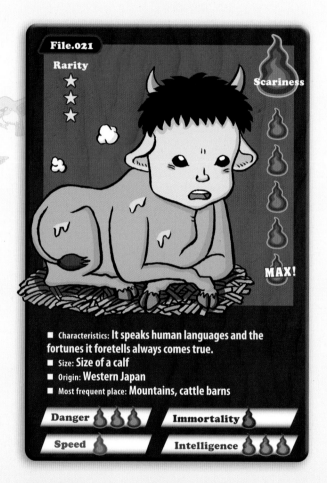

File.021

Rarity

★
★
★

Scariness

MAX!

- Characteristics: It speaks human languages and the fortunes it foretells always comes true.
- Size: Size of a calf
- Origin: Western Japan
- Most frequent place: Mountains, cattle barns

Danger

Immortality

Speed

Intelligence

Kudan is a Yokai with a human face and a cow body, and has been seen mainly in western Japan. It is said that Kudan speaks the language of humans and makes prophecies, which are guaranteed to come true.

However, the prophecies are often unfavorable, and Kudan seem to appear especially when there are major changes in the world, such as a crisis or war. Its lifespan is short, and it is said that he makes a prophecy as soon as it is born, and dies as soon as it makes its prediction.

Hitokusai (I-Smell-Human)

Sensitive to smell?! A single legged ghost that often appears in the mountain.

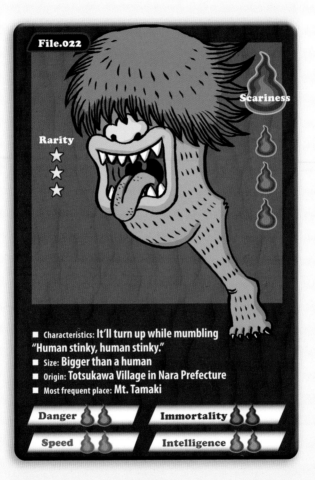

File.022

Scariness

Rarity
★
★
★

- Characteristics: It'll turn up while mumbling "Human stinky, human stinky."
- Size: Bigger than a human
- Origin: Totsukawa Village in Nara Prefecture
- Most frequent place: Mt. Tamaki

| Danger | | | Immortality | | |
| Speed | | | Intelligence | | |

Hitokusai is a ghost that appears in the mountains. It is said to be sensitive to smells, as it is said to approach peaple saying, "I smell human, I smell human." There is a story that a person who encountered a Hitokusai in the mountains was saved by a wolf who sheltered him. It is said to haunt a mountain called Mt. Tamaki in Totsukawa Village, Nara Prefecture.

This ghost has only one leg, but there is also a story of the one-legged Ippon-Datara. Perhaps the Hitokusai and the Ippon-Datara are related.

Chin Chin Kobakama

A ghost that looks a little like a young boy. At night, you'll find them coming at you while singing.

File.023

Rarity ★ ★ ★

Scariness

MAX!

- Characteristics: **A ghost that looks like a young boy with square face wearing a Hakama. They really enjoy singing.**
- Size: **Size of a toothpick**
- Origin: **Okayama and Oita Prefecture**
- Most frequent place: **Houses**

| Danger | | Immortality | |
| Speed | | Intelligence | |

The name Chin Chin Kobakama is said to be derived from a toothpick used to pick a cavity. There are stories of its existence on Sado Island in Niigata Prefecture, and in Okayama and Oita Prefectures.

One night, when the old woman was healed and spinning a thread, a boy with a square face and wearing a hakama (traditional Japanese male dress) appeared and disappeared, singing, "Chi-chi–hakama kiwakizashi wo sashite kore baa san nen nen ya."

The old lady was spooked by this and searched her home. She found a toothpick, which she burned and threw away, claiming that it cured her afterwards. It's a mystery why these little guys appear just to be burned away.

Otoroshi

A super mysterious thing that is just a ball of black hair with a scary expression.

File.024

Rarity
★

Scariness

MAX!

■ Characteristics: **A thing that's mostly a face covered with long black hair.**
■ Size: **Unknown** ■ Origin: **Unknown**
■ Most frequent place: **Unknown**

| Danger **?** | Immortality **?** |
| Speed **?** | Intelligence **?** |

Otoroshi is a ghost that is shrouded in mystery. It appears in an Edo period book called *Gazu Hyakki Yagyo*, which depicts a mysterious creature with a large mouth, nose, droopy eyes, three fingers, and its entire body covered in hair. However, there is no description of the mysterious creature, only a picture. So, we're not too sure what kind of Yokai it is exactly.

In Japanese, the word "otoroshi" means frightening. But in Nara and other dialects, the word "otoroi" means "troublesome." The depicted "otoroi" may look like a troublesome ghost, but it probably means a "frightening" ghost.

Shiri-Haguri

You'll find it in cemeteries around temples, rolling up its target's kimono showing its victim's butt.

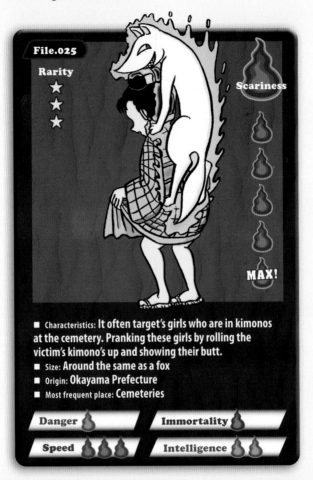

File.025

Rarity
★
★
★

Scariness

MAX!

- Characteristics: **It often target's girls who are in kimonos at the cemetery. Pranking these girls by rolling the victim's kimono's up and showing their butt.**
- Size: **Around the same as a fox**
- Origin: **Okayama Prefecture**
- Most frequent place: **Cemeteries**

Danger
Immortality
Speed
Intelligence

Shiri-Haguri is when the kimono rolls up and your buttocks are showing. However, legends say that the true identity of Shiri-Haguri is a fox that is attached to young girls.

One time, while the young girl was using the restroom in the cemetery of a temple called Toryin-ji, she accidentally peed on a fox that was taking a nap. The fox, wondering what she was thinking, became obsessed with the girl and began coming to the temple's cemetery and visiting the girl. In Japanese, the word "shiri" means butt, and "haguri" means to roll up the covering. We are not sure what he was trying to do, but I feel sorry for the girl who was possessed by the fox.

Sennenmogura (Thousand-Year-Old Mole)

A big white rare creature that looks like it doesn't belong in this world.

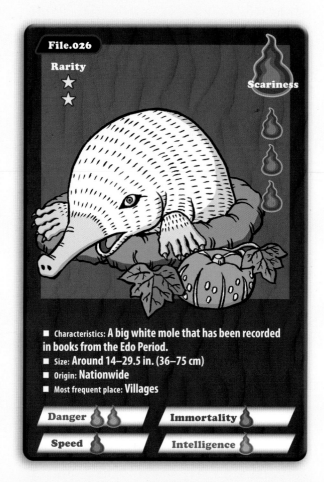

File.026

Rarity
★
★

Scariness

- Characteristics: **A big white mole that has been recorded in books from the Edo Period.**
- Size: **Around 14–29.5 in. (36–75 cm)**
- Origin: **Nationwide**
- Most frequent place: **Villages**

Danger	Immortality
Speed	Intelligence

The Sennenmogura is said to be a large mole-like creature, a thunder beast and also cholera.

In an Edo period book titled *Han-nichi kanwa*, there is a description of a large white mole that was caught, which was probably called a "sennen-mogura." It says that the size is about 14 in. (36 cm), and some even 29.5 in. (75 cm).

Some people have tried eating the Sennenmogura and found it delicious. It is quite a challenge to eat something that is also said to cause an illness such as cholera.

Kashambo

All of those who've seen it has different experiences. A mysterious being that appears in the mountains.

File.027

Rarity
★

Scariness

MAX!

- ▪ Characteristics: **The only thing people have in common about meeting KASHANBO is that they saw it in the mountains.**
- ▪ Size: **Somewhere between a child and an adult**
- ▪ Origin: **Wakayama and Mie Prefecture**
- ▪ Most frequent place: **Mountains**

Danger

Immortality

Speed

Intelligence

It is a thing that frequently appears in the mountains around Wakayama and Mie prefectures. Stories about Kashambo vary: "They don't look like humans, but they look like dogs,"

"Sometimes they are child-like things, and sometimes they are Yamamba with large breasts." Some say it is a Kappa that moved to the mountains because it likes to wrestle or pull humans into rivers to steal shirikodama(a mythical gem) from the human's butt. While others say it is a completely different thing from a Kappa.

Many stories have been passed down and we still have no further clues about Kashambo. And when mysterious footprints were discovered in Wakayama Prefecture in 2004, rumors spread that they belonged to Kashambo. The truth is also a mystery.

Makuragaeshi (Pillow Swapper)

A Yokai that appears at night and will mess with your sleeping posture.

File.028

Rarity
★
★
★

Scariness

- Characteristics: **It'll appear while people are sleeping and mess around with their posture.**
- Size: **About the same as humans**
- Origin: **Nationwide**
- Most frequent place: **Houses**

| Danger | | | |
| Speed | | | |

| Immortality | | | |
| Intelligence | | | |

Sometimes, when you wake up, you may find that your head and feet are turned in different directions from when you went to sleep. This may be the work of Makuragaeshi. It seems that Makuragaeshi sometimes appear in houses that have been built in places where they are not supposed to be. There is a theory that they are raccoons, monkeys, or haunted cats.

Incidentally, there is a monster that used to live in the Makuragaeshi called Makurakazou. It looks like a child and seems to be able to turn pillows of a sleeper or even bind them. It is quite unpleasant to have something done to you while you are sleeping without you noticing it!

Chinchirori

A Yokai that appears as a young brat. You'll find it on a mountain passes.

File.029

Scariness

Rarity
★
★
★

- Characteristics: **On your way home, you'll hear it calling you names.**
- Size: **Same as a child**
- Origin: **City of Iwakuni in Yamaguchi Prefecture**
- Most frequent place: **Mountain passes**

Danger		Immortality	
Speed		Intelligence	

Chinchirori is a ghost said to appear in Dosotoge in Iwakuni City, Yamaguchi Prefecture, and is recorded in the book *Iwakuni Kaidanroku*. The story went like this.

One day, Mr. Kato was returning home when he heard a voice calling out, "Kato-san wa chinchirori" (Mr. Kato is a chinchirori). When he turned around, he saw a ghost dressed like a little monk. When Mr. Kato replied, "That is exactly what I am" the ghost said again, "Kato-san is a chinchirori." The two continued to speak until finally they arrived at Mr. Kato's place. Chinchirori stood on the roof and laughed at Mr. Kato, saying, "You are a strong one, aren't you?"

Peroritaro (Licky Boy)

A Yokai born in the 20th century yet so old fashioned.

File.030

Rarity
★
★
★

Scariness

MAX!

- Characteristics: **Looks like a flabby child and eats greedy children.**
- Size: **Unknown** ■ Origin: **Unknown**
- Most frequent place: **Unknown**

Danger **?**   Immortality **?**

Speed **?**   Intelligence **?**

The Yokai known as Peroritaro suddenly appeared in the 20th century. It looks like a blubbering, flabby child and threatens to eat greedy children.

In the picture scroll "Hyakki Yagyo Emaki" from the Edo period (1603–1868), a very similar Yokai is called Ekataro, and it is probably the same one. It is a strange figure with a large face and a flabby belly. It has a squat jaw, a hanging tongue, and appears to be holding both hands almost or at the same time over its eyes.

Perhaps the character Bekataro in the "Hyakki Yagyo Emaki" was misread as Peroritaro.

Nurarihyon

The commander of Yokai's true form is mostly shrouded in mystery.

File.031

Rarity
★
★
★

Scariness

MAX!

- Characteristics: **Here he's taken form of an old man with a long back of the head.**
- Size: **About the same as humans**
- Origin: **Unknown** ▪ Most frequent place: **In the town**

Danger

Immortality

Speed

Intelligence

Nurarihyon is treated like a general of Yokai, but in fact, we don't know much about it.

In picture scrolls of the Edo period, such as "Hyakkai Zumaki," he is depicted as an old man with a long back of the head and a blue beard, but there is no written description of him. In a book titled *Saikaku 500 Rhymes*, also from the Edo period, there is a sentence that reads, "On a frosted autumn day, a white bearded man is relaxing." This is describing Nurarihyon and he seems to be just an old man.

Karasu Ojisan (Uncle Crow)

An old man that looks up to the sky and cries "KAW KAW!"

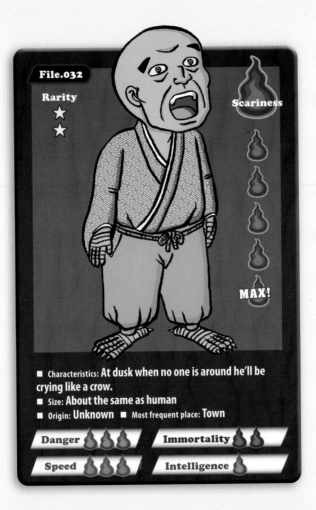

File.032

Rarity
★
★

Scariness

MAX!

- Characteristics: **At dusk when no one is around he'll be crying like a crow.**
- Size: **About the same as human**
- Origin: **Unknown** ■ Most frequent place: **Town**

| Danger | | | | Immortality | | |

| Speed | | | | Intelligence | |

Karasu Ojisan is just a ghost that stares at the sky and says "kaw-kaw-kaw." We aren't sure what for. He is said to appear in the evenings at places where no one is around.

No adult has ever seen him, and apparently only children can see him. If you are unlucky enough to encounter Karasu Ojisan, be careful. Never make eye contact with him. If you do make eye contact with him, he is said to chase after you. What in the world will happen if you get caught? No one seems to know.

Zashikiwarashi

She brings good fortune! A child ghost that appears in your home.

File.033

Rarity
★
★

Scariness

- Characteristics: **It is said that you'll start thriving if Zashikiwarashi appears in your home.**
- Size: **About the same as a child**
- Origin: **Nationwide**
- Most frequent place: **Houses**

Danger	Immortality
Speed	Intelligence

The Zashikiwarashi is a ghost of a child who lives in a house, and its gender is not fixed. They could be either a boy or a girl. Many stories are told in Iwate Prefecture and other parts of the Tohoku region. In Tono City, Iwate Prefecture, it is sometimes said that kappa and Zashikiwarashi are the same thing, or that kappa becomes Zashikiwarashi.

By entertaining a Zashikiwarashi, the family will prosper, and when it disappears, the family will fail. Zashikiwarashi is often thought of as a good thing that brings wealth, but it is not necessarily a good thing because bad things happen when it is gone.

Aburasumashi

A harmless ghost that always carry a container of oil for some reason.

File.034

Rarity
★
★
★

Scariness

MAX!

- ■ Characteristics: **It holds a container of oil and will appear at mountain trails. It understands human languages.**
- ■ Size: **Unknown**
- ■ Origin: **Kumamoto Prefecture**
- ■ Most frequent place: **Mountain trails**

Danger	Immortality
Speed	**Intelligence**

It is said that Aburasumashi is a ghost that appears on the mountain path with a bottle of oil, but the details are not well known. According to the book *Amakusa Shimanchu Zokushi*, an old lady was walking her grandson along a place called Kusadoregoe when she remembered the story of the Aburasumashi. When the grandmother told her grandson, "Koko ni yatashi yorai tachi yuzo (Here, they say, a lowered oil bottle appeared in the past)," he went and came out, saying, "It still appears today." But, perhaps she just wanted to show her presence, she only startled them but did not do them any great harm.

The Mountain Pass Where Nakanekozou Appears

Nakane Pass, where the mountains meet.

Driving from Nara City toward Wakayama, you will arrive at Shimokitayama Village. It takes about two and a half hours to get from Nara City to Shimokitayama Village, even if you drive smoothly. If it is your first

Nakane Pass, Nara Prefecture, Shimokita-Yamamura, Ikemine

visit, you will need a lot of courage. However, since southern Nara Prefecture is green and has no traffic lights, you will enjoy a pleasant road trip. For those who cannot drive, there is a bus service from Kintetsu Yamato-kamiichi Station, but it takes quite some time even to get to the station. It is recommended to have someone else drive you.

The village was once famous during the Tsuchinoko boom of the Showa period (1926–1989). A mini-independent country called the "Republic of Tsuchinoko" was created and people from inside and outside the prefecture were invited to move there. In such a village, there are not only tales of the earthly creatures, but also stories of the Nakanekozou (page 42).

The mountain pass where the Nakanekozou are said to appear does exist. There is also a Jizo (a stone statue) that is said to point to the pass, although it seems to have been placed there only after the Nakanekozou was killed. It is possible to see it for oneself if one climbs the mountain, but it is not recommended for those who are not accustomed to hiking mountains to do so alone, as it is considered too dangerous. It is best to start by just gingerly looking around the mountain pass.

According to the villagers, there was indeed a festival held to appease the evil of Nakanekozou. However, the exact number of years was not known, and it was not clear when the festival was held and for how long.

Kazuo Nozaki, the chairman of the Tsuchinoko Republic in the village, said, "In the past, the area around Nakane Pass was a road for daily life. My mother actually used that road to come and go in the village." He told us that his mother actually used that road to go to and from the village.

Nakane Pass is where the Yamatoya
area overlaps and is hollowed out.

Chapter 3

Super Powerful Yokai

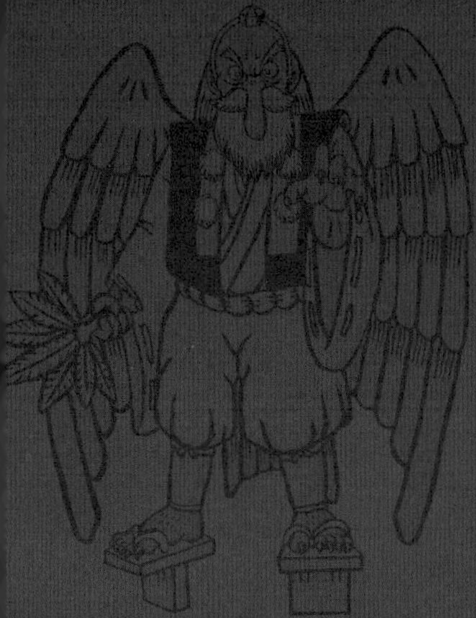

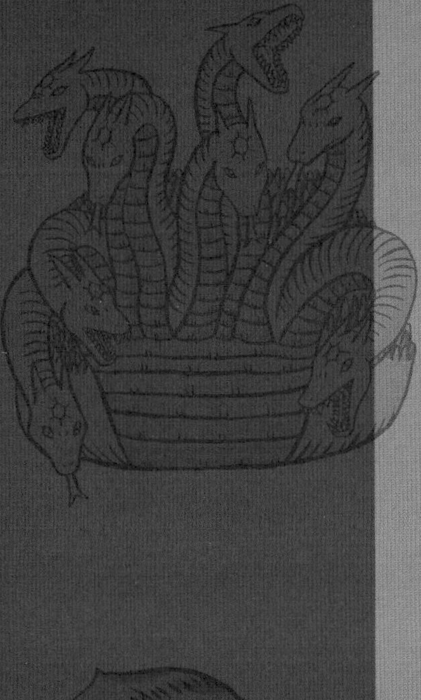

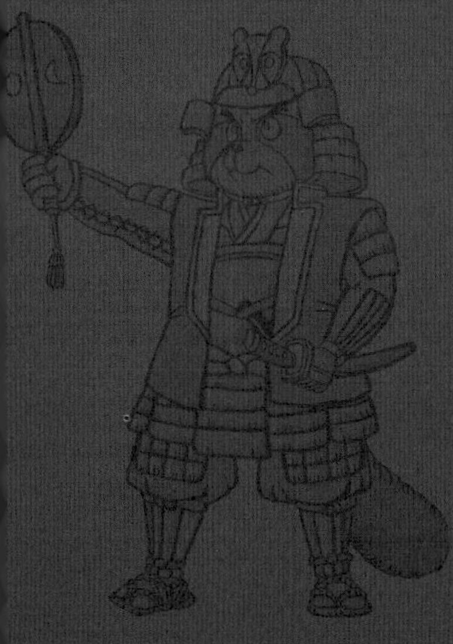

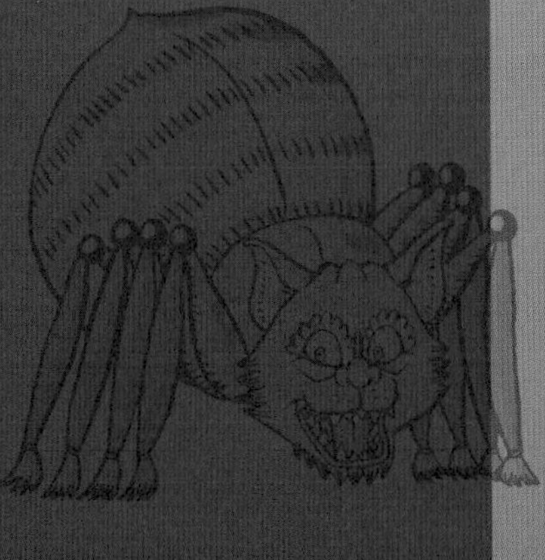

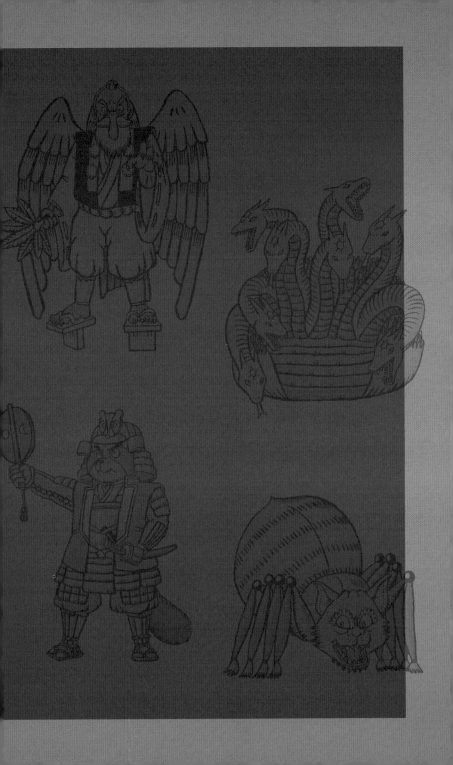

Yamata no Orochi

The legendary giant stage spirit that even appears in Japanese Mythology.

File.035

Scariness

Rarity
★
★
★

MAX!

- **Characteristics:** It has 8 heads and 8 tails and will kidnap people.
- **Size:** The size of 8 mountains and 8 valleys combined
- **Origin:** Shimane Prefecture, Hokuriku Region
- **Most frequent place:** Around humans

Danger	Immortality
Speed	Intelligence

The Yamata no-Orochi is a giant serpent that appears in the *Kojiki* and *Nihonshoki*. It is known to have confronted Susanoo-no-Mikoto, the child of Izanagi and Izanami, the gods who created Japan.

Mythology describes it as having eight heads and eight tails, and its eyes were like red demon lanterns. Pine trees and oaks grew on his back and moss, and his body was the size of eight hills and eight valleys. Every year, he would sacrifice one human being to eat, but he fell for Susanoo-no-Mikoto's scheming and was finally overthrown. It is still enshrined at Atsuta Shrine today.

This is SUPER Strong!

🔥 **Its size is the span of 8 hills and 8 valleys combined**

▶ 8 heads and 8 tails

▶ Gem-like red eyes

▶ Pines and oaks grow on its mossy back

Interesting Fact

Yamata no Orochi is a monster of great scale who fought against Susanoo no Mikoto, the child of Izanagi and Izanami, the Shinto deities who created Japan.

Ushioni (Ox Demon)

It LOVES to scare people and often appears along coastlines and brings calamity.

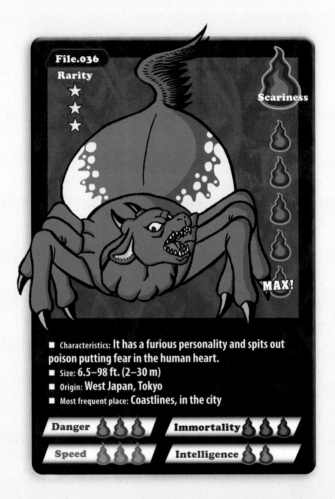

File.036
Rarity
★
★
★

Scariness

MAX!

- Characteristics: **It has a furious personality and spits out poison putting fear in the human heart.**
- Size: **6.5–98 ft. (2–30 m)**
- Origin: **West Japan, Tokyo**
- Most frequent place: **Coastlines, in the city**

| Danger | | | | Immortality | | | |
| Speed | | | | Intelligence | | |

Ushioni, known as terribly ferocious ghosts, are said to appear frequently in coastal areas of western Japan.

There seem to be several types...one has a head like an ox and a body like an ogre from the neck down. On the other hand, there's also kinds with a head like an ogre and a body like an ox. Some have a body like a Tsuchigumo (page 71). They are said to be feared by people because of their large size and the calamity they bring.

Because they kill and haunt people, there are festivals and shrines throughout Japan to appease the spirits of the Ushioni demons.

This is SUPER Strong!

🔥 You'll find that the names of some places in the Kinki and Shikoku regions are name after Ushioni

▶ It has a cow's head. You'll sometimes find Ushioni with human head too.

▶ It has a spider body. Sometimes you'll find ones with a human body.

▶ It spits poison from its mouth and loves eating humans.

Interesting Fact

There is also a legend about an ox demon that can make a person sick just by encountering it.

Akaragashira

No one can stop it from running away! It can devour a whole field.

File.037

Rarity
★
★
★

Scariness

- **Characteristics:** It rarely makes an appearance. It's a beast with a red face.
- **Size:** A little bigger than the ordinary wild boar
- **Origin:** City of Tenri in Nara Prefecture
- **Most frequent place:** Fields

Danger	Immortality
Speed	**Intelligence**

The word "akara" in Akaragashira is thought to mean the same thing as "Red Face." It is a beast-like ghost found in fields around Tenri City, Nara Prefecture.

It lurks deep in the mountains and rarely appears in public. But on the first day of the eleventh lunar month, a cold day, Akara appears and eats everything in the wild in just one day. The villagers were so frightened that on November 11, they made offerings and prayed that Akara would not attack them.

It is said that it was a large boar-like creature, but the truth is unknown.

Kincho-Tanuki

A righteous and powerful being! A commander of a Tanuki War.

File.038

Scariness

Rarity
★

- Characteristics: **A Tanuki spirit that doesn't like to be indebted to humans.**
- Size: **About the same as a Tanuki**
- Origin: **Tokushima Prefecture**
- Most frequent place: **Near Humans**

Danger		Immortality	
Speed		Intelligence	

Kincho-Tanuki is a ghost Tanuki that played an active role in the Awa Tanuki War.

At one time, the Tanuki leader Kanenaga was employed by Rokuemon Tanuki Nomoto in order to raise his rank. Rokuemon, recognizing Kanenaga's growing power, tried to persuade him to follow in his footsteps as his son-in-law. However, Kanenaga refused, which angered Rokuemon, attacking him in the middle of the night. After risking their lives, Kincho and Rokuemon led their respective clans to war, and Kincho's righteous and hardworking way of life has captured the hearts of many people.

Shutendoji

A strong and smart alcohol-loving demon leader.

File.039

Rarity

Scariness

MAX!

- Characteristics: A very smart demon leader that gathers a lot of demons together.
- Size: About the same as a human
- Origin: Sanin, Sanki Region
- Most frequent place: Capital, caves

Danger

Immortality

Speed

Intelligence

Shutendoji was the leader of the demons, who controlled a large number of demons. He lived on Mt. Oe in Kyoto and was known for his love of alcohol.

There are many stories, most of them are about how Shutendoji, a demon, was attacked in his sleep and exterminated by a warlord named Miyaki no Yorimitsu who came from the capital. Because of their high intelligence and physical strength, such as his being able to converse with humans, they may have been seen as very dangerous.

Tsuchigumo

A spirit that takes the form of a spider. It is said that it eats humans.

File.040

Rarity
★
★
★

Scariness

MAX!

- Characteristics: **A large spider spirit that is plotting to take over the world.**
- Size: **3–6.5 ft. (1–2 m)** ■ Origin: **Nara, Kyoto**
- Most frequent place: **Mansions**

Danger	Immortality
Speed	Intelligence

Tsuchigumo was an ancient derogatory name for the indigenous people who did not obey the power of the central government. Over time, it came to appear frequently in stories as a ghost in the form of a spider.

The most famous of these is probably "Tsuchigumo Zoshi Emaki." It is a story about a giant spider defeated by Minamoto no Yorimitsu. When he took the head of the spider, many skulls were said to have come out from inside its belly. Minamoto no Yorimitsu was the military commander who defeated Shutendouji.

There remains a "Tsuchigumo mound" at the Itsukunushi Shrine in Nara, where he is said to have buried a Tsuchigumo.

Tamamonomae

A master of Dark Magic. She is smart and beautiful. The ultimate beauty.

File.041

Rarity
★
★
★

Scariness

MAX!

- **Characteristics:** Disguises as a court lady to enter the imperial court and capture the emperor.
- **Size:** About the same as a human
- **Origin:** Kyoto metropolitan area and Tochigi Prefecture
- **Most frequent place:** Imperial court, mountains

Danger	Immortality
Speed	Intelligence

Tamamomae is a beautiful courtesan who is an incarnation of a golden-haired nine-tailed fox. The nine-tailed fox is a Yokai that appears in Chinese mythology.

During the Heian period, there was a courtesan named Tamamo-mae. She was not only beautiful but also smart, and became beloved by Emperor Toba, who supported her. However, when the emperor eventually discovered that Tamamomae was the culprit behind an illness of unknown cause, the courtesan turned into a nine-tailed fox and fled. The imperial court led a troop to exterminate the nine-tailed fox, but she played tricks on the humans with her beauty, intelligence, and sorcery.

Tengu

Sometimes he'll fight, sometimes he'll help. An unpredictable Yokai.

File.042

Rarity

Scariness

- Characteristics: **It lives deep in the mountains, dressed like a mountain priest.**
- Size: **About the same as a human**
- Origin: **Nationwide**
- Most frequent place: **Mountains**

Danger	Immortality
Speed	Intelligence

The Tengu is one of the most well-known Yokai, with tales of its existence spanning throughout the country. As Buddhism flourished in Japan, the Tengu came to be seen as a strong obstacle to Buddhism, something that would fight monks. The word Tengu is said to have been introduced from China. In any case, it was a natural phenomenon beyond the power of man.

Nowadays, Tengu have a strong image of a red face with a long nose, but before the Edo period, the Tengu was portrayed more like a bird.

Temple Where the "Tengu Apology" Was Received

Butsugen-ji Temple
Shizuoka prefecture, Toushi,
Monomigaoka 2-30
0557(37) 2177

Butsugen-ji Temple—where stories
about Tengu are handed down

Take the JR train from Atami, go south and get off at Ito Station. In front of the station, you will see many specialty stores selling dried seafood. Take a bus from the station, and after a while you will arrive at the bus stop nearest the Butsugen-ji Temple. It is said that there was once a monk named Nichian Shonin at this temple. It is said that around the first year of Manji (1658), a Tengu annoyed people at a mountain pass called Kashiwa Pass in Amagi.

When Nichian Shonin appointed a priest there, a scroll was thrown down from a pine tree which contained an apology from the Tengu for bothering people. Since then, the Tengu have not been seen. The problem, however, is the characters written on the scroll were very mysterious.

The actual "Tengu's Apology" is still carefully preserved at a museum. It is not open to the public, but we were given a special opportunity to view it. As we opened the scroll, which was over 10 ft. 5 in. (3.13 m) long, we were

Difficult to decipher Tengu Apology Letter

Yokai Report Shizuoka Prefecture
(Butsugen-ji Temple)

Information board on Tengu lore
in the precincts of the temple

Tengu apology yokan made by
Tamaya, a Japanese confectionery
shop

surprised. Indeed, I could not understand what it said at all. Some of the characters looked like Chinese characters when turned upside down, but I still had no idea what they meant...a strange array of characters.

The temple staff told us, "We have tried to decipher them with the help of researchers, but in the end, we still don't know what they mean. Will someone be able to decipher them in the future?"

We hope you will give it a try, too.

The back of the yokan package shows a part
of the Tengu apology and its origin

Chapter 4

Super Weird Yokai

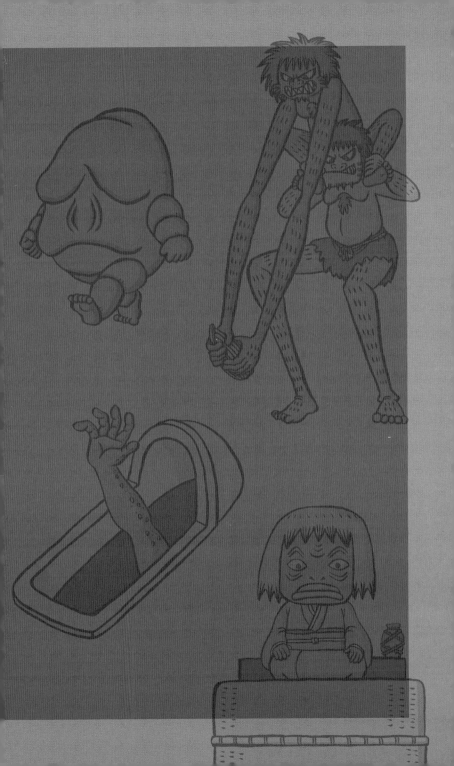

Tenaga-Ashinaga (Long-Limbed Giants)

Siblings? A married couple? A weird giant that appears as a pair.

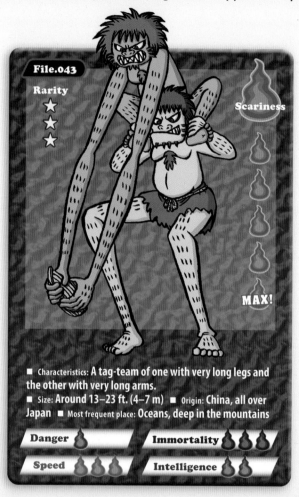

File.043

Rarity
★
★
★

Scariness

MAX!

- Characteristics: **A tag-team of one with very long legs and the other with very long arms.**
- Size: **Around 13–23 ft. (4–7 m)** ■ Origin: **China, all over Japan** ■ Most frequent place: **Oceans, deep in the mountains**

Danger		Immortality	
Speed		Intelligence	

As the name implies, Tenaga-Ashinaga meaning "long-limbed giants" have very long arms and legs. There are horror stories of them attacking people who are traveling and ships crossing the sea, taking people and eating them.

In the ancient Chinese book *Shan Hai Jing*, aliens called "long-armed" and "long-legged" appear. Were these the model for the Japanese "Tenaga-Ashinaga?" They also have various faces, such as being worshiped as gods. Although different from these giants, a book called *The Pillow Book* from the Heian period (794–1185) mentions that there was a shoji (sliding door) depicting a long-hand and long-legged man inside a palace. What does this have to do with Tenaga-Ashinaga? No one knows!

This is SUPER Weird!

💡 A tag team of one with super long legs and the other with super long arms

▶ A pair of siblings, but some also indicate their relationship is marriage

▶ Ashinaga appeared alone in the Edo period book called Koshi Yawa (Night Tales of Koshi). There, the length of its foot is said to be about 9 ft. (2.7 m).

Interesting Fact

Some say that they belong to a race of footmen and to the Fotatsu tribe of the Choujin, and that they fish in teams at sea.

Tenome (Eye Hands)

Its eyes are not on its face… but its hands!? An elderly ghost that'll appear in town.

File.044

Rarity
★
★

Scariness

MAX!

- **Characteristics:** It'll pretend to be a blind person. The moment it spots a person, it'll follow them.
- **Size:** About the size of a large person
- **Origin:** West Japan, Tokyo
- **Most frequent place:** Towns

| Danger | | Immortality | | | |
| Speed | | | Intelligence | | |

As the name suggests, "te (hands) no me (eyes)" is a ghost with eyes in the palms of its hands. It appears in an Edo period book called *Gazu Hyakki Yagyo* (*One Hundred Demon Nights*). In the book, there is a picture of a blue ghost with no eyes, and a blue ghost with eyes in the palms of its hands, as if it were showing them to someone.

In *Gazu Hyakki Yagyo* there is a story about a man whose bones were pulled out by a monster. In the story, it is written that a monster with eyes in the palms of its hands appeared in a cemetery in Shichijo Kawara, Kyoto. It was an old man with a large body. Tenome in *Gazu Hyakki Yagyo* may have been modeled after the monster in "Hyakumonogatari."

This is SUPER Weird!

It's rumored in Kyoto that he appears at a grave.

▶ It appears to resemble a Zato

▶ It'll turn its palm with eyes towards whatever it wants to look at

Interesting Fact

Zato is a blind biwa (a stringed instrument) player. People who sing while playing the koto or shamisen, or who work in needlework, are sometimes called Zato.

Kainade

It'll grab your butt in the toilet? A ghost that no one wants to meet!

File.045

Scariness

Rarity
★
★

MAX!

■ Characteristics: **A ghost that appears in the restroom and will touch whoever sits on the toilet.**
■ Size: **Unknown**
■ Origin: **Kinki Area**
■ Most frequent place: **Restrooms**

Danger

Immortality

Speed

Intelligence

Kainade is a ghost that goes out to the bathroom and pats people on the butt. It is said to appear on the night of Setsubun (the day before Spring).

Kainade is probably written with the literal meaning "scratching and patting" in Japanese. The story seems to be told mainly in Kyoto. It is said that if you do not want Kainade to stroke your buttocks, you should say, "Red hair or white paper?" There is also a story that when you go to the bathroom in the middle of the night, you have to bow your head and say, "I will not come tomorrow."

Nuppepo

Where does the head end and the body start? It's pretty much a giant head with folded flesh all around.

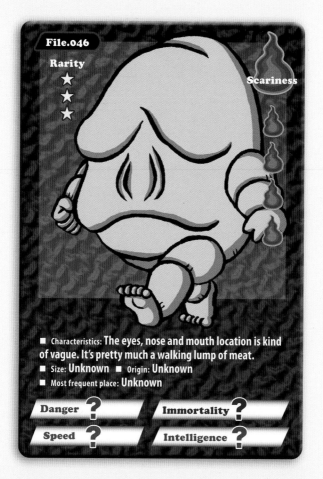

File.046

Rarity
★
★
★

Scariness

- Characteristics: The eyes, nose and mouth location is kind of vague. It's pretty much a walking lump of meat.
- Size: Unknown ■ Origin: Unknown
- Most frequent place: Unknown

| Danger | ? | Immortality | ? |
| Speed | ? | Intelligence | ? |

Nupeppo is a stocky, full-bodied ghost that looks like a lump of meat. From what is depicted, it seems to have eyes, a nose, a mouth, and some sort of arms and legs, but details are not clear.

Nuppehou appears in an Edo period book titled *Gazu Hyakki Yagyo* (*One Hundred Demon Nights*), where it is depicted together with a fishing bell. Later, it came to be said that Nupe-ho "appears at abandoned temples and other places," which may have been associated with the picture in *Gazu Hyakki Yagyo*.

From the sound of the name, Nuppeho could also be considered a member of the Noppebo family.

Otekurebaba (Piggy-Back-Ride-Me Granny)

An old granny ghost that'll suddenly hop on your back at night.

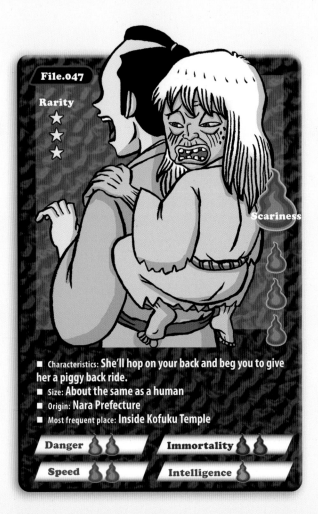

File.047

Rarity

★
★
★

Scariness

- Characteristics: **She'll hop on your back and beg you to give her a piggy back ride.**
- Size: **About the same as a human**
- Origin: **Nara Prefecture**
- Most frequent place: **Inside Kofuku Temple**

Danger	Immortality
Speed	**Intelligence**

Outekurebaba is a ghost of an old woman who suddenly comes running after you from behind, saying, "Give me a piggy back ride!" It is said to appear mainly in Nara Prefecture. At Kofuku-ji Temple in Nara Prefecture, it is said that if you walk around the Hokuendo and the Sanjyu-do area at night, you will see Outekurebaba. If you go around the three-story pagoda three times and throw stones at it, they may come out from inside. If you accidentally carry it on your back, it may bite you on the head.

Another ghost called "Obariyon" from Niigata Prefecture is said to be similar to Outekurebaba, and will also suddenly climb onto your back.

Keukegen

A stubborn hair Yokai that is rarely seen.

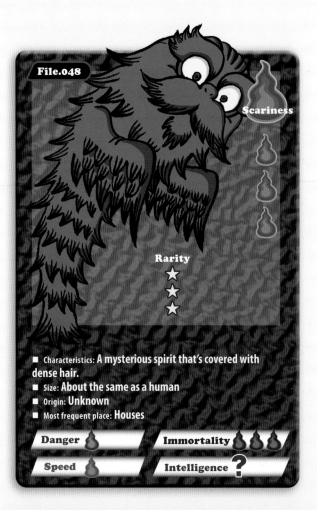

File.048

Scariness

Rarity
★
★
★

- Characteristics: **A mysterious spirit that's covered with dense hair.**
- Size: **About the same as a human**
- Origin: **Unknown**
- Most frequent place: **Houses**

Danger

Immortality

Speed

Intelligence ?

Keukegen is a ghost covered with a lot of hair, and although it seems to have eyes, it is so hairy that it is doubtful if it can see at all. In an old Chinese book, there is a hermit called "Mao Nyonna" who is covered with hair all over her body, and Keukegen is sometimes compared to her.

We don't know exactly what they are, but from what we have seen in paintings, they seem to appear in the vicinity of houses. Dust and hairballs sometimes appear from the corners of rooms that have not been cleaned, but could that be a Keukegen?

Nandobaba (Storage Room Granny)

A old lady spirit that'll appear in unused storage rooms.

File.049

Rarity
★
★

Scariness

- Characteristics: **You'll hear her sigh in a storage room.**
- Size: **About the same as a human**
- Origin: **Okayama Prefecture**
- Most frequent place: **Storage room**

Danger

Immortality

Speed

Intelligence

Do you have a storage room in your house? Perhaps there is a "Nandobaba" there, a ghost in the form of an old woman. According to a story from Akaban County, Okayama Prefecture (now Akaban City), a bald-headed old woman is said to come out of the closet saying, "Ho!" If you hit her with a broom, she will run away under the porch. She does not seem to be doing anything evil, but it is eerie because we do not know her purpose.

Chirami Kozo (Lurking Brat)

A pure hearted brat that lurks in the shadows peeping at humans.

File.050

Rarity
★
★

Scariness

- Characteristics: **It'll lurk in the shadows while staring at you.**
- Size: **About a size of a human child**
- Origin: **Unknown**
- Most frequent place: **Shadows**

Danger

Immortality

Speed

Intelligence

Chirami Kozo is a ghost that hides in shadows and glances at you. It is said that when it finds someone doing something wrong, it tries to let people know by secretly whispering about it. Basically, it does not like to make contact with people. It lives in shady or quiet places, and is always on the lookout for human activity. He is always watching people, perhaps wanting to get a little closer to hear what they are saying.

Yokai Questions

Question 2

The other day I saw a Yokai on TV.
Is it real?

I don't know what kind of TV programs you've seen but you will find something like it in every possible program. TV programs are made by people, therefore, the Yokai that appear on TV are not real. However, it is believed that the people who make TV programs are creating Yokai-like beings based on real records. For those who are concerned about whether the stories are real or not, read about Yokai and create your own opinion.

Question
3

I honestly don't want to meet any Yokai. Please tell me how to avoid meeting them.

There are some people who really want to meet Yokai, and there are others who never want to. I think the best way to deal with this is "if you don't feel it, you don't believe it." Avoid thinking about Yokai. Tell yourself you want to never meet one and you won't.

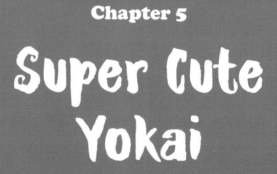

Chapter 5

Super Cute Yokai

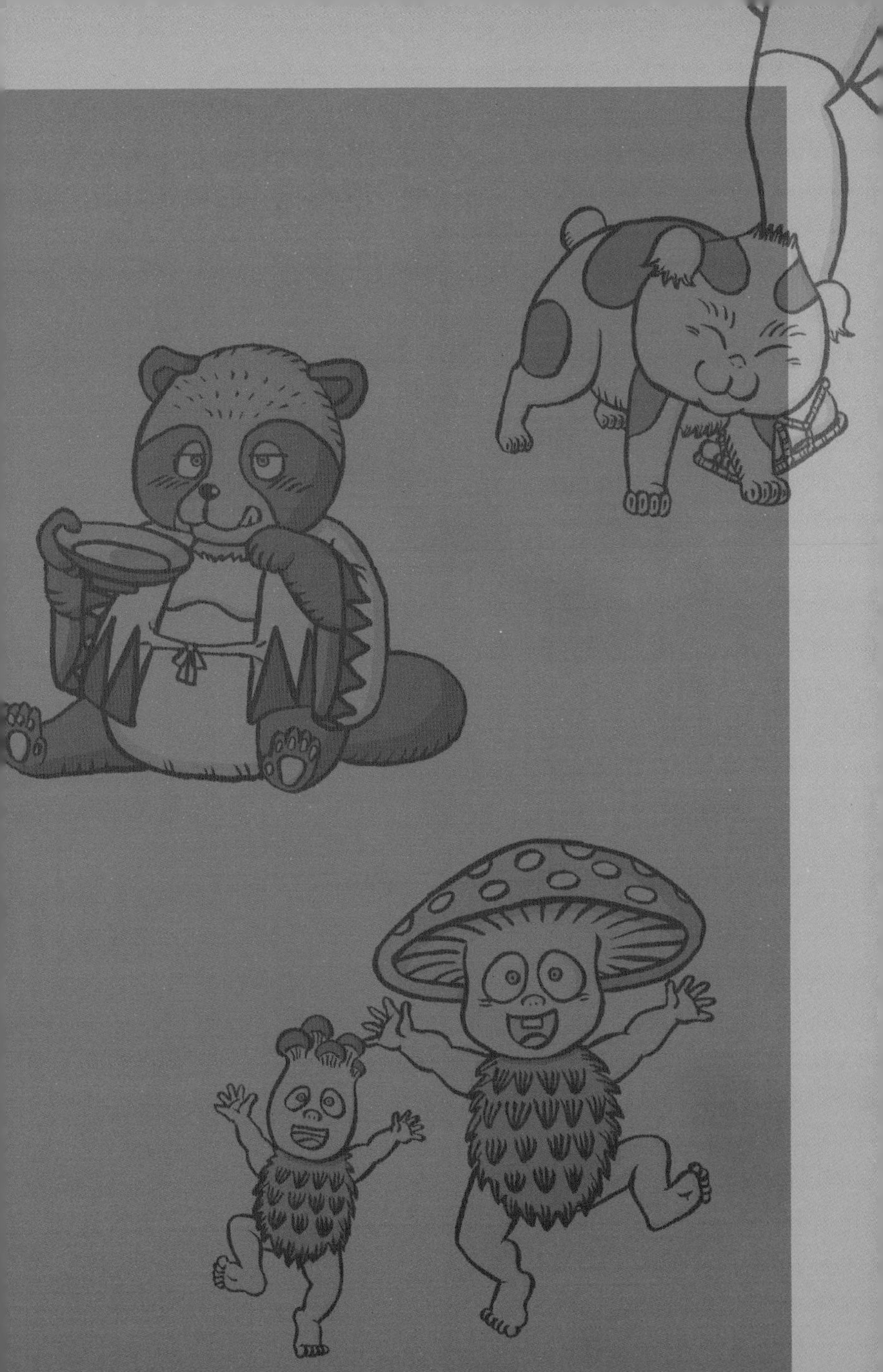

Betobetosan (Mr. Sticky)

You'll sense it steadily follow you from behind but you can't see it!

File.051

Rarity
★

Scariness

MAX!

- Characteristics: **You'll often sense him from behind while walking outside at night.**
- Size: **Unknown**
- Origin: **Nara, Shizuoka Prefecture**
- Most frequent place: **Outside at night**

Danger	Immortality
Speed	Intelligence

When you are walking alone at night, if you feel like someone is following you, there is sure to be Betobetosan there. Betobetosan will not do anything in particular except follow behind you. If you are worried about it, you can stop by the side of the road and say, "Betobetosan, go ahead," and you will not feel it anymore. It may be that it is afraid to walk alone.

There is a ghost similar to this called Bishagatsuku. It is said that when walking in bad winter weather, one hears footsteps that sound like "bishabisha-bishabisha." If you only hear the sound, it sounds more energetic than Bishagatuku.

This is SUPER Cute!

- It steadily follows you from behind.

- If you tell it to go ahead, you'll stop feeling it behind you.

▶ This face is invisible to you

▶ Based on the sound it makes when walking, we think that it has on some shoes

Interesting Fact

Invisible to the eye, yet there is a presence. Mr. Betobeto projects a sensation you can feel as you walk.

Kusabira

Children that'll appear in the mountains. It's actually a mushroom god!

File.052

Rarity
★
★
★

Scariness

MAX!

- **Characteristics:** It's a kind of Yamawaro (one eyed monster) that looks like a mushroom. It enjoys helping humans.
- **Size:** About the same as a human child
- **Origin:** Kinki Region
- **Most frequent place:** Mountains

Danger

Immortality

Speed

Intelligence

Kusabira is a ghost that lives in the mountains and looks like a child. It originally referred to a mushroom, and is sometimes worshipped as a deity who saves people from starvation and death. In addition to Kusabira, Nara Prefecture also has a story about a ghost called "Ki-no-Ko," or "tree child." The "Ki no Ko" looks like a 3–4 year old child with teeth on its body. Both Kusabira and Ki-no-Ko are said to be a type of Yamawaea Kusabira.

This is SUPER Cute!

💧 It's probably a kind of Yamawara

▶ They'll help you with mountain work and help those who're lost and starving in the mountains.

▶ They look like children.

▶ Its body is covered with leaves.

💧 **Interesting Fact** 💧

It's also been said that Kusabira sometimes emit a blue light once night falls. If you see the light in the mountains, it may be Kusarabi.

Notabozu

It loves drinking too much! A Tanuki spirit that's always drunk.

File.053

Rarity
★
★
★

Scariness

- Characteristics: It wears a back and white haori and hangs around a sake brewery.
- Size: About a size of a Tanuki
- Origin: Aichi Prefecture
- Most frequent place: Sake breweries

Danger
Speed
Immortality
Intelligence

The Notabozu is an old raccoon dog that disguises itself as a person. He is said to wear a black-and-white dandara-patterned cloak, enter a sake brewery, and drink the sake that is fermenting.

One day, Notabozu was caught, but was forgiven on the promise that he would not steal anything in the future and that he would make the house where he returned the sake prosperous. He must have been quite a sake lover to go all the way into a brewery and drink sake that was still fermenting. Or perhaps he was just a drunkard. A drunk person is called a "notamakunin" (a drunkard), but what does the "nota" in "notabozu" mean?

Sunekosuri

It'll come up to your shin and start rubbing against it like a dog.

File.054

Rarity
★
★

Scariness

MAX!

- Characteristics: It looks like a dog and often appears on a night that's raining.
- Size: About the size of a dog or cat
- Origin: Okayama Prefecture
- Most frequent place: Outside at night

| Danger | |
| Speed | |

| Immortality | |
| Intelligence | |

Sunekosuri is a spirit that rubs its way between the legs of people walking by. It has a body like a dog and is said to appear on rainy nights. There are many stories about it in Oda-gun, Okayama Prefecture.

It is said to be a gentle ghost that sometimes does not harm people. However, if a dog-like creature passes by my feet on a rainy day, I feel that I would get soaked to the skin. Unfortunately, there is no information about what to do if you really don't want to get wet, or any countermeasures. If you don't want to meet them, it is better not to go outside on a rainy day.

Sodehikikozo (Sleeve Tugging Brat)

It wants your attention. A spirit that'll tug on your sleeves while you're walking.

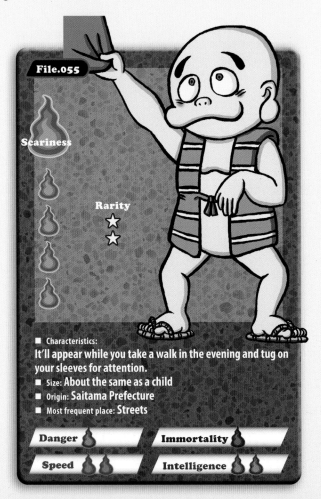

File.055

Scariness

Rarity
★
★

■ Characteristics:
It'll appear while you take a walk in the evening and tug on your sleeves for attention.
■ Size: About the same as a child
■ Origin: Saitama Prefecture
■ Most frequent place: Streets

Danger	Immortality
Speed	Intelligence

As you walk down the street in the evening, you feel a tug on the sleeve of your garment. At such times, there may be a "sleeve-pulling boy" next to you. In the days when Japanese people wore kimono, they would have had no trouble with their sleeves. However, modern dress has made it a little more difficult to pull back the sleeves, and although we cannot be sure what Sodehikikozo is thinking about, we hope that there will be more opportunities for it in the future.

Kijimuna

A unique spirit that resides on an old ficus tree.

File.056

Rarity
★
★

Scariness

- **Characteristics:** There are male and female Kajimunas. They each rest on their own ficus tree.
- **Size:** From a size of a bird to a size of a ficus tree
- **Origin:** Okinawa Prefecture
- **Most frequent place:** All around Okinawa island

| Danger | 🔥🔥 | Immortality | 🔥🔥 |
| Speed | 🔥🔥🔥 | Intelligence | 🔥🔥🔥 |

Kijimuna is a kind of bird that is said to dwell in old trees such as ficus trees.

There are various stories about its red face, red hair, and bright red body. They are also said to have a male and female gender.

They are all said to have different personalities, and each Kijimuna has its own personality. Some do nothing, some join with others to fish. Many stories related to fire are also told.

Yokai Questions

Question 4

When I see a bad Yokai, I would like to protect myself. Is there a good way to do this?

It is cool if you can protect yourself from an attacking Yokai at the spur of the moment. You will definitely be a hero at school. However, danger can come suddenly. It would be nice if you were lucky enough to have a club, but it may not work out that way. So this time, we will teach you a method that may allow you to easily repel a Yokai...even if you are unarmed.

All you have to do is to spit on them. That's all. It seems that more than a few Yokai are averse to human saliva. Each Yokai has different weaknesses, but the only thing you can do easily is to spit on them.

Incidentally, if you encounter a Yokai, leave it alone. People and Yokai live in different worlds. It is better not to think of bringing them back home and trying to be friends with them.

Chapter 6

Super Simple Yokai

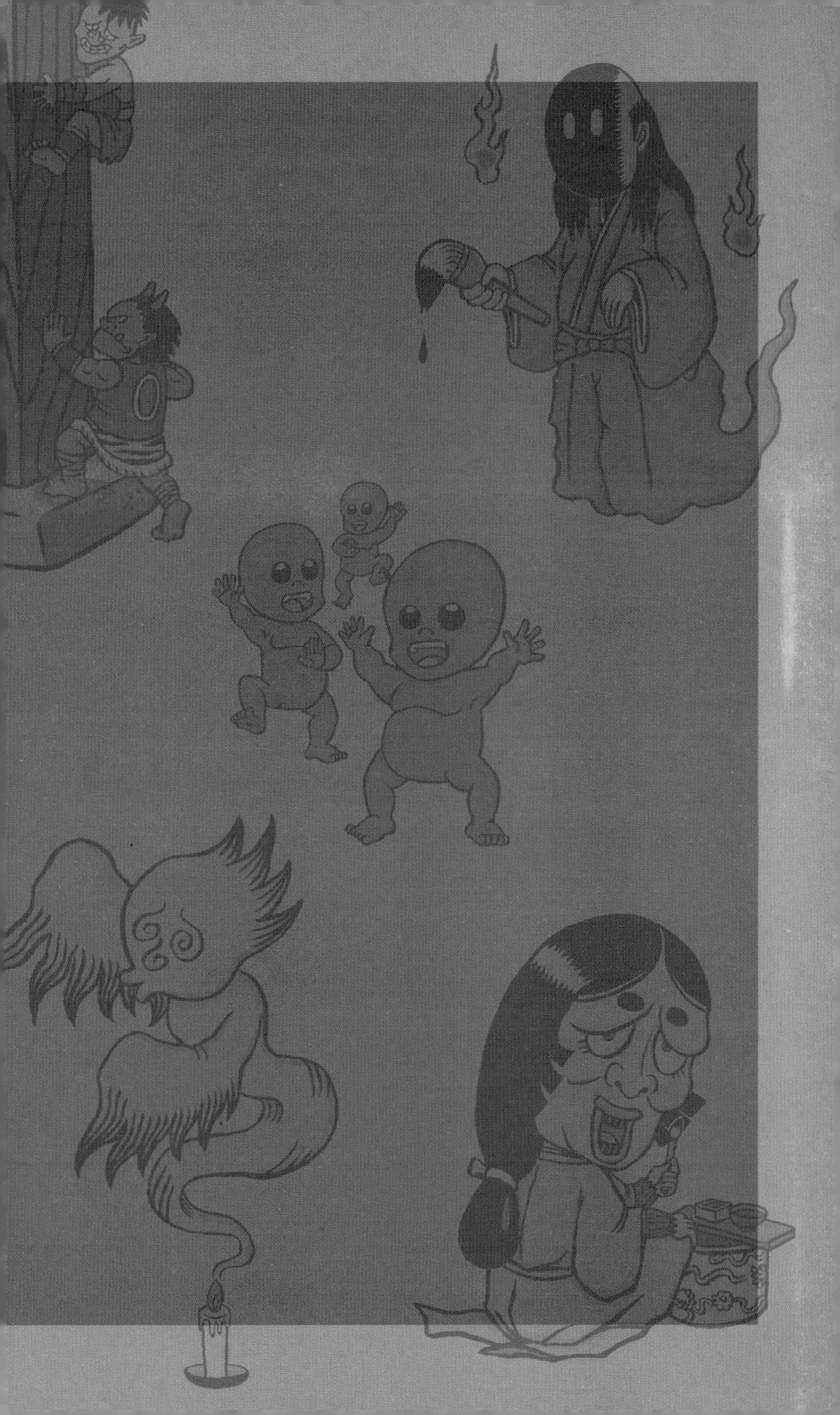

Sumitsuke (Painter)

A ghost that died holding a grudge. Its revenge is to mark people with ink.

File.057

Rarity

Scariness

MAX!

- Characteristics:
It'll appear at night and mark bypassers with ink.
- Size: About the same as a human
- Origin: Hyogo Prefecture
- Most frequent place: Outside at night

Danger

Immortality

Speed

Intelligence

It is said that Sumitsuke are Samurai ghosts who smear ink on passersby every night in Aioi City, Hyogo Prefecture.

There was a castle that once existed in Doshi called Kanjozan Castle. It is said that some warriors tried to invade the castle. However, it seems that he could not get in successfully, and he died. The Sumitsuke is said to be the ghost of these Samurai. It is a sorry ghost.

It doesn't seem to do anything in particular other than to put ink on people's body.

Nurikabe (Painted Wall)

An annoying ghost that'll block the road as a prank.

File.058

Rarity
★
★
★

Scariness

- Characteristics: **It'll suddenly appear to block your way at night.**
- Size: **Unknown**
- Origin: **Kyushu Region**
- Most frequent place: **Outside at night**

Danger

Speed

Immortality

Intelligence

Nurikabe appears suddenly when people are walking along a street at night, blocking their passage. The story is told in the Kyushu region, including Onga-gun, Fukuoka Prefecture.

If you encounter one, it is best to use a stick to brush it off at the bottom. It seems to be a specter that is rather easy to counteract.

In recent years, Nurikabe, which look like three-eyed animals, have been found painted on picture scrolls and have become a topic of conversation. However, it is not known at this time whether this is the same thing as the painted wall that blocks the road.

Akakgo (Baby)

A toddler ghost that's completely red. It'll dance and smile all night until the morning.

File.059

Scariness

Rarity
★
★
★

- Characteristics: It'll disguise itself as a baby. Its entire body is red.
- Size: Toddler size
- Origin: Nara, Nagano Prefecture
- Most frequent place: The room next door, underwater

Danger

Immortality

Speed

Intelligence

Akago are similar to newborn babies. The number of Akago is increasing rapidly, and although they look like human beings of 11 or 12 years of age, they are colored bright red. A book titled *Haunted Picture Scrolls* from the Meiji period (1868–1912) records a story about a scroll in Nara. There are more than a dozen bright red creatures painted on the scroll, and they seem to be dancing. They seem to be smiling and happy. These babies are said to have disappeared at dawn.

Ao Nyobo (Blue Lady)

A court lady doing her makeup in a ruined castle waiting for someone.

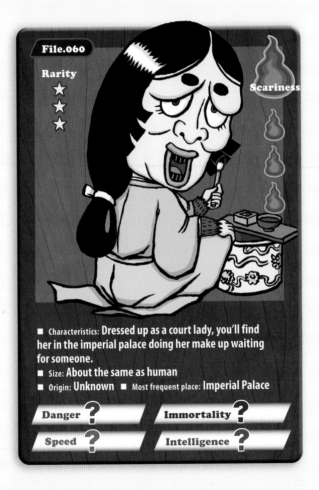

File.060

Rarity
★
★
★

Scariness

- **Characteristics:** Dressed up as a court lady, you'll find her in the imperial palace doing her make up waiting for someone.
- **Size:** About the same as human
- **Origin:** Unknown ■ **Most frequent place:** Imperial Palace

| Danger | ? | Immortality | ? |
| Speed | ? | Intelligence | ? |

The Ao nyobo is a ghost in the form of a courtesan. Ao nyobo appears in an Edo period book titled *Konjaku gazu zoku hyakki*, in which she is depicted with bushy eyebrows and a long coat of hair. She is said to be waiting for someone to visit her in her dilapidated palace, while applying her make-up incessantly.

What happened to Ao nyobo that made her wait so long for someone to visit her? The more I think about it, the more I can't help but imagine how sad it must have been for Ao nyobo, and I hope someone wonderful will come to visit her.

Oshiroi-Baba (Powder Granny)

A granny ghost that wanders the street with her white powdered face.

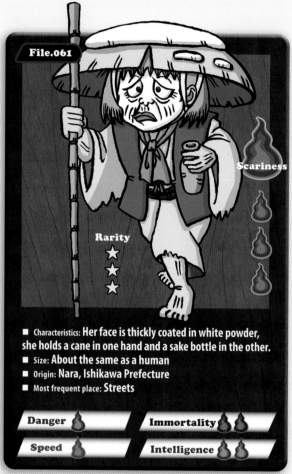

File.061

Scariness

Rarity
★
★
★

- ■ Characteristics: **Her face is thickly coated in white powder, she holds a cane in one hand and a sake bottle in the other.**
- ■ Size: **About the same as a human**
- ■ Origin: **Nara, Ishikawa Prefecture**
- ■ Most frequent place: **Streets**

Danger	Immortality
Speed	Intelligence

Oshiroi-Baba is said to be the ghost of an old lady, appearing dragging a mirror or begging travelers for white powder. Stories have been handed down in Nara and Ishikawa prefectures.

In an Edo period book titled *Imaon Hyakki Jiken* (*Imaon Hyakki Pickup Book*), an old lady Oshiroi-Baba, appears wearing a hat and holding a walking stick and a sake bottle in her hand. According to the explanation written here, Oshiroi-Baba is apparently a temple maiden of God.

In the vicinity of Hase-ji Temple in Nara Prefecture, it is said that Oshiroi-Baba was once a daughter who took care of the monks at the temple, and after hardships she became an old woman.

Yanari

When you hear a mysterious squeak in the house, could it be from these tiny demons?

File.062

Rarity
★

Scariness

- ■ Characteristics: **Without any particular reason, these guys make little squeaks in your house.**
- ■ Size: **Unknown**
- ■ Origin: **Nationwide**
- ■ Most frequent place: **Basements**

| Danger | | Immortality | |
| Speed | | Intelligence | |

When the house starts to squeak or shake for no reason, you may say, "This is Yanari's fault." In the Edo period book *Gazu Hyakki Yagyo*, a small demon-like creature is depicted shaking the house. If your house is shaken by such an adorable thing, you cannot hate it.

A house may also become when something bad happens, such as when a person dies. Is it a sign or a reflection of the feelings of those who live there? Even if a ghost cannot be seen, if there is a sound, we can sense its presence.

Yosuzume (Night Sparrow)

Actually a forewarning of bad luck? They're little bird spirits that chirp all night.

File.063

Scariness

Rarity ★

- Characteristics: **It'll chirp chirp chirp all night long.**
- Size: **About the size of a regular sparrow**
- Origin: **Shikoku Region**
- Most frequent place: **Villages**

| Danger | Speed | Immortality | Intelligence |

At night you hear chirp chirp chirp. This may be the cry of "Yosuzume Night Sparrows." They fly into the night while crying.

You might think, "It's so plain. Isn't it just a bird?" But be aware, it is not just any bird. It may have played a role in foretelling bad luck. Depending on the region, to repel the bad luck it is beneficial to chant "Do birds that cry chi, chi, chi, yearn for a shinagi rod, and if they do, then let them be struck with a single blow" or "Birds that cry chi, chi, chi, please let the divine wind of Ise swiftly blow you away."

Enenra

An evolving mosquito repellant!

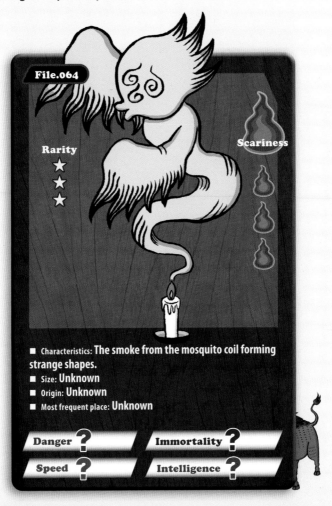

File.064

Rarity
★
★
★

Scariness

■ Characteristics: The smoke from the mosquito coil forming strange shapes.
■ Size: **Unknown**
■ Origin: **Unknown**
■ Most frequent place: **Unknown**

| Danger **?** | Immortality **?** |
| Speed **?** | Intelligence **?** |

Enenra is an unusual smoke ghost.

So far, no story has been found that has been passed down among the people. It seems to have been handed down to the present based on a picture and description in an Edo period book titled Hyakki Yagyoi. The book's description reads, "The smoke that was smoked to drive away mosquitoes had a mysterious shape," and it depicts a smoke monster shaped like a human face. In this light, Enenra may be a kind of evolution of mosquito coils.

Hohonade (Cheek Rubber)

It'll suddenly start rubbing your cheeks. So simple yet disturbing.

File.065

Scariness

Rarity

- Characteristics: **It'll appear on small roads and try to rub bypasser cheeks.**
- Size: **Unknown**
- Origin: **Tokyo, Yamanashi Prefecture**
- Most frequent place: **Small roads**

Danger

Immortality

Speed

Intelligence

It is strange thing, a pale hand that comes out and caresses your cheek as you walk down the path. The figure is often invisible and the hand seems cold.

Anyone would be startled by a sudden touch on the cheek by something unknown.

There is a story that in Tokyo, this weird thing that strokes one's cheek could be a leaf or a long blade of grass. And some say the touch leaves a cut that bleeds. It's a mystery we may never solve.

Kamaitachi

It appears with the wind and start cutting you.

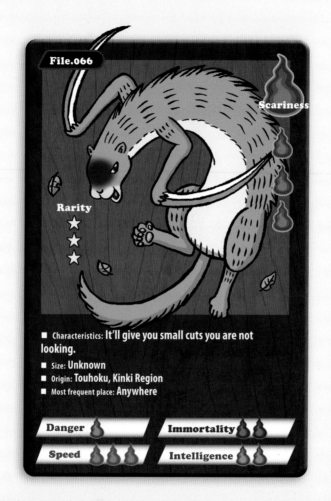

File.066

Scariness

Rarity

★
★
★

- **Characteristics:** It'll give you small cuts you are not looking.
- **Size:** Unknown
- **Origin:** Touhoku, Kinki Region
- **Most frequent place:** Anywhere

| Danger | 🌢 | | Immortality | 🌢🌢 |
| Speed | 🌢🌢🌢 | | Intelligence | 🌢🌢 |

Kamaitachi are good at making small cuts on arms and legs. It is sometimes called Kamae-tachi or Kamaittachi.

They often appear with a cold, and some say that they act in groups of three. In such cases, it seems that the roles of the three animals are divided: one pushes down, one cuts, and one applies medicine. I don't know what in the world they are trying to do, but perhaps it is their job to wound, even if only for a moment.

Question 5

There are scary stories of ghosts at school. Are these Yokai?

School ghost stories were very popular even back when I was a child. That was more than 20 years ago. I remember that the most popular ones around at the time were "the human-faced dog," "the slit-mouthed woman," and "the purple hag." These were the ones that appeared on the way to school. It was not unusual to actually see suspicious people on the way to school, so this may have had something to do with it. In the beginning, scary school stories may have been nothing more than mysterious things that happened at school. However, as time went by and various legends, histories, and local tales were added, they may have gradually become Yokai.

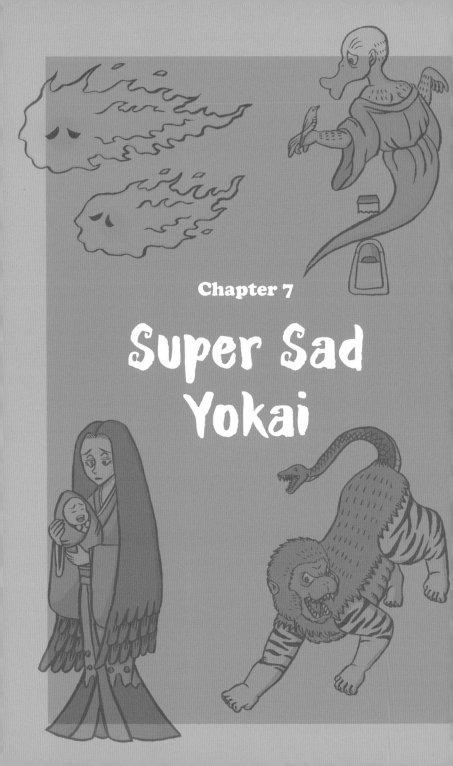

Chapter 7

Super Sad Yokai

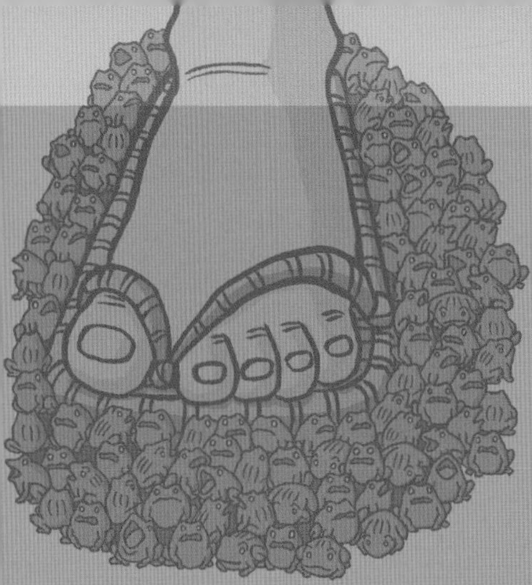
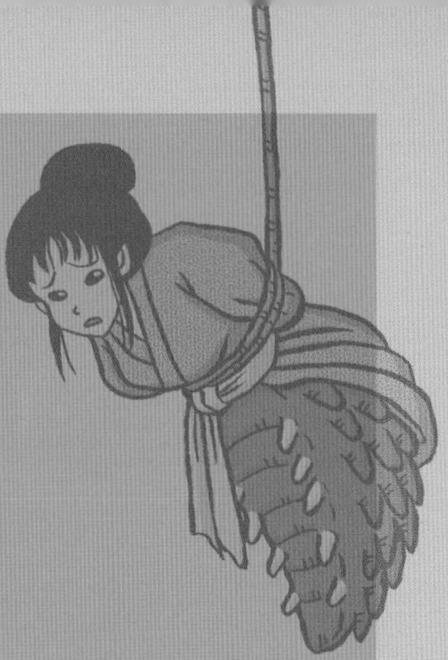
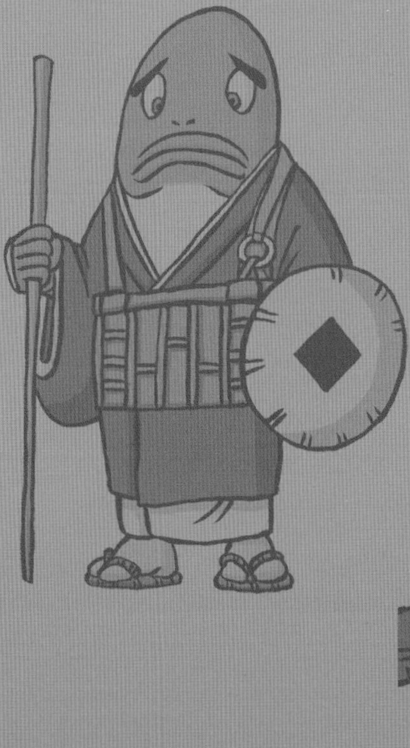
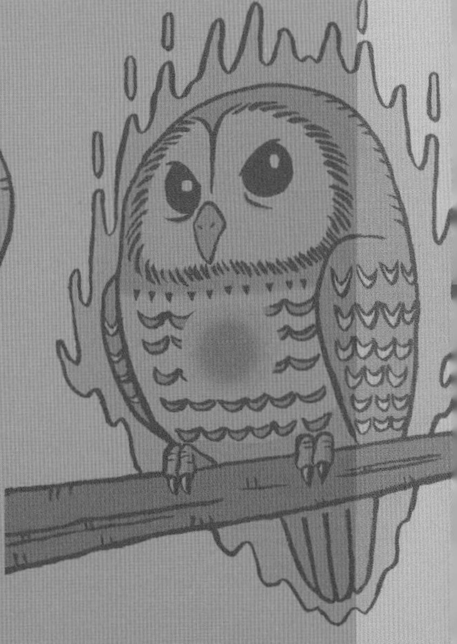

Nue

A Yokai that has a frightening appearance but is truly just a sad creature.

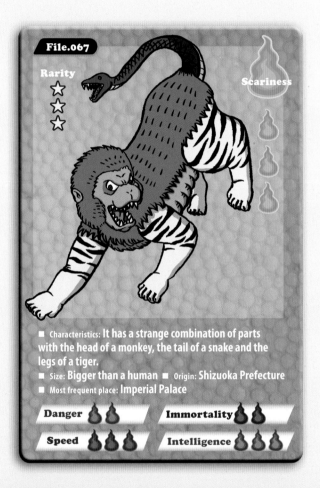

File.067

Rarity
★
★
★

Scariness

- Characteristics: **It has a strange combination of parts with the head of a monkey, the tail of a snake and the legs of a tiger.**
- Size: **Bigger than a human** ■ Origin: **Shizuoka Prefecture**
- Most frequent place: **Imperial Palace**

Danger	Immortality
Speed	Intelligence

Nue has the bizarre appearance of a monkey's head, snake's tail, and tiger's legs. It is said to have been exterminated by a warlord named Minamoto no Yorimasa because it annoyed the emperor with its forlorn cries at night. The story is told in Kyoto, where the capital was located, as well as in many other places. It is recorded in the *Kojiki* (Records of Ancient Matters) and *Manyoshu* (Anthology of Myriad Leaves) from the Nara period (710–794), making it one of the oldest Yokai. The Nue that appears in the old records has come to be feared and is reported to bring misfortune.

This is SUPER Sad!

Nue is a terrifying Yokai with a pitiful story.

▶ Snake's tail

▶ Tiger's limbs

▶ Monkey's head

Interesting Fact

The Nue is an ancient Yokai. Known for its mournful cries, it seems to have a very lonely existence.

Ganborinyudo

It appears in the bathroom on New Year's Eve, spitting birds out of his mouth.

File.068

Scariness

Rarity

■ Characteristics:
He appears in the bathroom on New Year's Eve just to scare people.
■ Size: A little bigger than humans
■ Origin: Nation wide
■ Most frequent place: Restroom

Danger

Immortality

Speed

Intelligence

Ganborinyudo is a ghost that appears in toilets. An Edo period book titled *Konjaku gazu zoku hyakki*, or *One Hundred Demons of the Edo Period*, depicts it as noisily growing hair and vomiting birds from its mouth. However, there is also a legend that if you utter the words "Ganborinyudo Hottogisu" on New Year's Eve, bad things will happen.

In the book *Rengoku Kaidan Henshocho* by Jippensha Ikku, the ghost is said to be a fox, and it meets an untimely and sad end when it is bitten to death by a dog.

This is SUPER Sad!

💧 Apparently it died as a result of a dog bite.

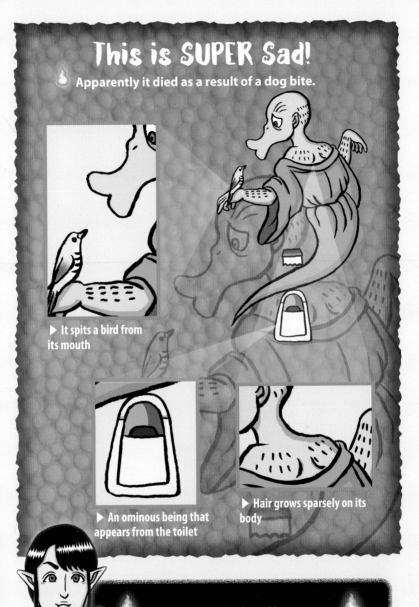

▶ It spits a bird from its mouth

▶ An ominous being that appears from the toilet

▶ Hair grows sparsely on its body

Interesting Fact

In the past, the restrooms were dark, so it was an eerie place that feels like anything can show up at any time. Because of this, many probably avoid going to the restroom alone.

Janjanbi

The souls of a man and a woman who were heartbroken? A suspicious fire involving in death.

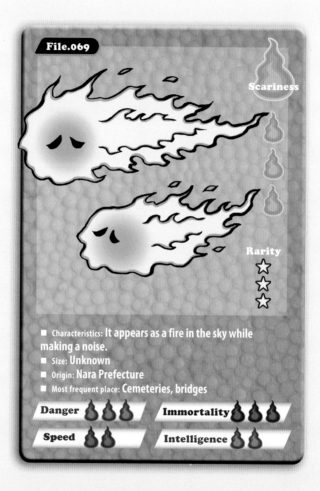

File.069

Scariness

Rarity

- Characteristics: It appears as a fire in the sky while making a noise.
- Size: Unknown
- Origin: Nara Prefecture
- Most frequent place: Cemeteries, bridges

Danger

Immortality

Speed

Intelligence

Janjanbi is a mysterious fire that makes a jang-jang sound. It is said to be the souls of a man and woman who have been betrayed or the spirit of a Samurai who has been killed in battle, and is often the result of people's sadness. In Nara Prefecture, there are Hoihoihi and Zannenbi, which are similar to these mysterious fires. There is also a story that if you call out "hoihoi" to them, they will come and disappear while making a "janjan" sound.

If you see it, you may be bedridden with a fever for two or three days.

Okikumushi

A pupa tied to a pillar! Related to one of the most famous hauntings in Japan.

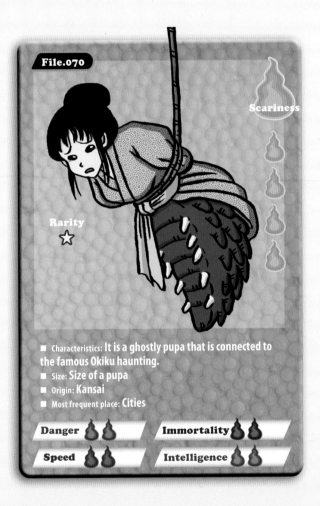

File.070

Scariness

Rarity
☆

■ Characteristics: It is a ghostly pupa that is connected to the famous Okiku haunting.
■ Size: Size of a pupa
■ Origin: Kansai
■ Most frequent place: Cities

Danger

Immortality

Speed

Intelligence

Have you ever heard of the story "Bancho Sarayashiki?" It is a ghost story about a girl named Okiku who was killed and became a ghost after being beaten by her master for breaking a plate. One of these "Okiku legends" passed down is the story of girl who, after her death, emerges not as a ghost but as an insect called Okikumushi and is tied to a pillar.

In Himeji, Okikumushi were sold as souvenirs until around the beginning of the Showa period (1926–1989).

Mokurikokuri

This little guy has a tragic past. A ghost that appears near water.

File.071

Rarity
☆ ☆ ☆

Scariness

- Characteristics: **It's known as Mokuri Gokuri, known to generally be fearful.**
- Size: **Unknown**
- Origin: **Nationwide coastline**
- Most frequent place: **By the coast, in the mountains**

Danger 🔥🔥		**Immortality** 🔥🔥	
Speed 🔥🔥		**Intelligence** 🔥🔥	

There are many stories about Mokurikokuri. Some say it looks like a weasel and attacks the buttocks of those who enter wheat fields at night, others say it looks like a jellyfish and drifts at sea in groups, and still others say it is the soul of someone who has drowned.

It is said that if you enter the mountains on March 3 in Wakayama Prefecture, Mokurikokuri will appear.

Tatarimokke

The spirit of someone who was killed in a terrible way. It haunts those guilty of murder and the people around them.

File.072

Rarity ☆☆☆

Scariness

MAX!

- Characteristics: **You'll hear an owl crying when it appears.**
- Size: **Unknown** ■ Origin: **Aomori Prefecture**
- Most frequent place: **Outdoors**

Danger 💩💩

Immortality 💩💩💩

Speed 💩💩💩

Intelligence 💩💩

A person who has been brutally killed uses the power of their grudge to curse the person they killed and the people around them. This urban legend is often told in Aomori prefecture. The "mokke" part of its name is another way of saying "mononoke" meaning ghost in Japanese. In the Aomori dialect, it seems to refer to frogs.

In some regions, a newborn baby is likened to a frog, and in Goshogawara, the spirit of a dead baby is called 'Tatarimokke,' and it is said that Tama City dwells in an owl. In the past, children were sometimes killed because families were too poor to afford them. It must have been very difficult for both the child and the parent.

Iwanabouzu

Even though it helps warn people about pointless killing, in the end, it's the one that gets eaten.

File.073

Rarity ☆☆☆

Scariness

MAX!

- ■ Characteristics: **Borrowing a monk's attire, it tries to warn fishermen against pointless killing.**
- ■ Size: **Same as a human**
- ■ Origin: **Gifu Prefecture**
- ■ Most frequent place: **Riversides**

Danger	🌶	**Immortality**	🌶	
Speed	🌶	**Intelligence**	🌶🌶🌶	

Iwanabouzu is said to be a river fish disguised as a man, who appears in deep mountain rivers to warn people who are catching fish.

It also appears in an Edo period book titled *Souzan Shokubun Kishu* (*The Book of Souzan Books*). It is not a bad thing, but it is a monster that tries to stop people from killing fish in the village. The people who are warned of the monster succeed in driving it away by serving it a meal. Later, when a large fish is caught and its stomach is opened, the fisherman just might see the meal they fed to the Iwanabouzu. It seems that their actions are never rewarded.

Soroban Bozu (Abacus Boy)

A ghost of a small monk who appears at temples and shrines and plays with an abacus.

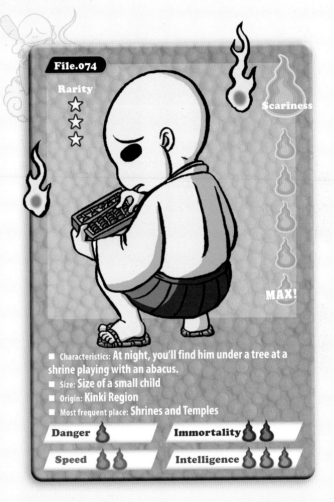

File.074

Rarity
☆
☆
☆

Scariness
MAX!

- Characteristics: At night, you'll find him under a tree at a shrine playing with an abacus.
- Size: Size of a small child
- Origin: Kinki Region
- Most frequent place: Shrines and Temples

Danger

Immortality

Speed

Intelligence

These are ghosts that play the abacus under the trees of temples and shrines late at night. Stories of Soroban Bozu are told in Kameoka City in Kyoto and other places.

Some believe it is a Tanuki, while others believe it to be the last of the little monks at the temple. There is a story that the little monk made a mistake in his calculations, which angered the monk, and he died after being hanged.

Everyone makes mistakes in calculations. Was he so serious or was the monk's scolding too severe that he died because he was told of his mistake? Either way, it is a pity.

Ubume

An unbelievably sad tale of a woman who died during childbirth.

File.075

Rarity
★
★
★

Scariness

- Characteristics: **You'll find her on the streets at night holding a baby. If she finds you, she'll make you hold the baby.**
- Size: **About the same as a human**
- Origin: **Nationwide** ■ Most frequent place: **Outside at night**

| Danger | 🍐🍐🍐 | Immortality | 🍐🍐🍐 |
| Speed | 🍐🍐🍐 | Intelligence | 🍐🍐 |

Ubume is a woman who died during childbirth. It is said that she cries with her baby in her arms at night on the street and makes people she meets hold her child in their arms...too sad a story to tell.

In a Heian-period book titled *Konjaku Monogatari-shu*, there is a story about a man who tries to cross a river and is almost forced to carry a baby in his arms by Ubume. It seems that the story of Ubume has remained deep in people's hearts since ancient times.

San no Maru-Gaeru (Castle Outskirt Frogs)

The grief of those who were sentenced to be decapitated, packed in these small bodies.

File.076

Rarity
☆
☆
☆

Scariness

- Characteristics: **They're very tiny. During rainy season, they'll appear in masses.**
- Size: **Approximately 0.1 in. (3 mm)**
- Origin: **Koriyama, Nara Prefecture**
- Most frequent place: **Outskirts of Koriyama Castle**

Danger	Immortality
Speed	Intelligence

This is a very small frog that appears during the rainy season. It is said that it got its name from its appearance in the San no Maru area of Koriyama Castle in Koriyama City, Nara Prefecture. The most striking feature of the frog is its size. It is said that tens of thousands of these small frogs appear out of nowhere.

According to a passage, they are said to be the delusions of people who were decapitated in the past, and their small bodies must be filled with sadness.

Shrines that Helped Exterminate Nue

"Nue-Daimyoujin," a shrine quietly located in Nijo Park

Not far from Nijo Castle, in a corner of Nijo Park, "Nue-Daimyoujin," a shrine dedicated to Nue, quietly stands. It was a weekday when I visited, and the park was crowded with children, businessmen who were probably killing time, and tourists. At first glance, it looked like a typical

Nue Daimyoujin Shrine
Kyoto, Kamigyou-ku
Chiekouindo-ri Maruta-choukudaru
Shuzei-chou 964

park, and not many people seemed to notice that Nue-daimyoujin was located there. When we inquired at Kyoto City Hall, we were told that the shrine is currently managed by a local resident. The shrine is well cared for, and it is evident that it has been carefully protected.

As mentioned earlier, the Nue was a nuisance to the emperor and was exterminated by the warlord Minamoto no Yorimasa (page 118) There is a pond beside the shrine, which is called Nue Pond. It is said to be the place where a Nue was killed and where

In front of the shrine, there you'll see Nue Pond

Minamoto no Yorimasa washed the arrowhead he used when he killed it. This pond is also said to have been restored as when the park was renovated. It is now a U-shaped pond with a tree planted in the center.

Incidentally, although it is some distance away from Nue-daimyoujin, there is a shrine called Shinmei-jinja Shrine (Shinmei-cho, Shimogyo-ku, Kyoto City, Kyoto Prefecture) that was toppled by a Nue.

It is said that Minamoto no Yorimasa, after praying at the shrine, went out to kill the Nue and was able to defeat it successfully.

Nue's grave stone

Chapter 8

Super Kind Yokai

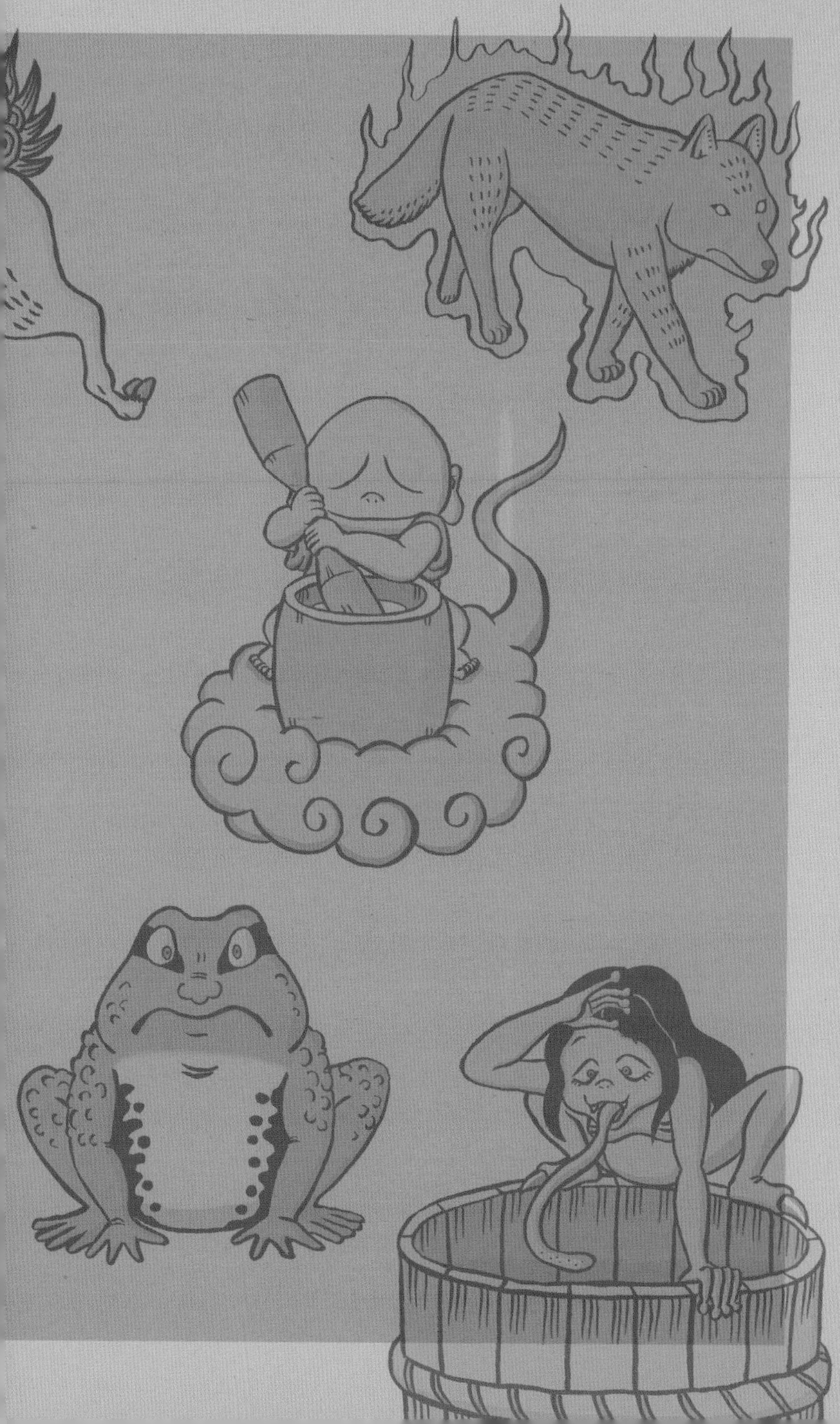

Hakutaku

A divine beast from China that appears before the best and most respectable people.

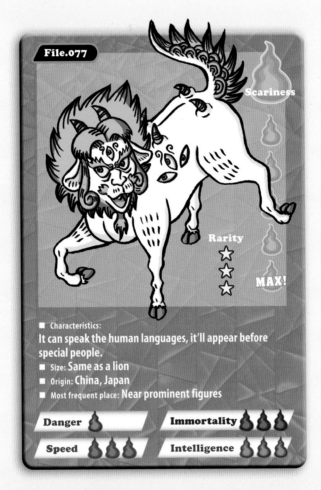

File.077

Scariness

Rarity
★
★
★

MAX!

■ Characteristics:
It can speak the human languages, it'll appear before special people.
■ Size: Same as a lion
■ Origin: China, Japan
■ Most frequent place: Near prominent figures

Danger

Immortality

Speed

Intelligence

Hakutaku is a legend from mainland China, and is a divine beast that appears to a king with virtue. Later, it came to be worshiped as a god of Chinese medicine.

Hakutaku was introduced from China, but in Japan, it began to appear in printed materials around the Edo period (1603–1867) and became widely known. According to a book of the same period called *Wakan sansai zue*, it is said to appear in front of a person who is virtuous and respectable. There are also recorded stories of people in ancient China who were able to avoid harm through the advice of Hakutaku.

This is SUPER Kind!

💧 It was introduced to China in ancient times and is said to have the power to prevent misfortune.

▶ It looks similar to a lion

▶ It may look like a beast, but it speaks human languages

Interesting Fact

It is often mistaken with Paku (page 143). It's a being that can cure illness, a painting of it is often used as a good luck charm.

Kamikiri (Haircutter)

A ghost that'll appear in the middle of the night to cut your hair.

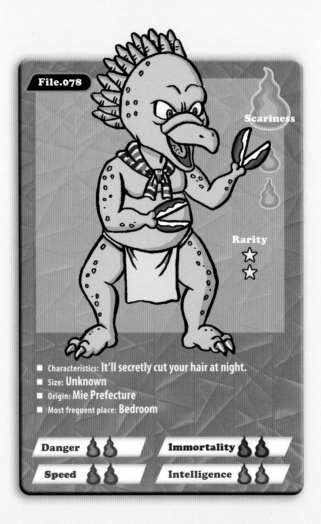

File.078

Scariness

Rarity ☆☆

- **Characteristics:** It'll secretly cut your hair at night.
- **Size:** Unknown
- **Origin:** Mie Prefecture
- **Most frequent place:** Bedroom

Danger	Immortality
Speed	Intelligence

Kamikiri is a ghost that appears in the world and secretly cuts people's hair.

It may have been especially popular in the Edo period (1603–1867), and appears frequently in records of the Edo period (1603–1868). It is a bit creepy, but it is a good deal because you can save money on a haircut! However, it is usually women who gets them. There is a story that it is named after an insect called a hair cutter, but there are also many theories that it is a fox.

This is SUPER Kind!

💡 Its true form is unknown, but some say it may look like a fox.

▶ In the book *Hyakkaizukan*, it is depicted with a beak

▶ It'll cut human hair at night

Interesting Fact

The true form is said to be a fox or an insect called a kamikiri bug. I wonder if the stories may have actually been about people secretly cutting someone's hair as they slept. In any case, I would be very grateful if I could get a nice hair cut for free!

Akaname (Grime Licker)

It seems kind of gross, but it actually likes to lick up all the grime in the bath.

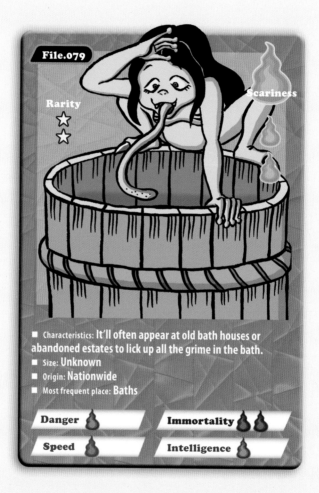

File.079

Rarity ☆☆

Scariness

- **Characteristics:** It'll often appear at old bath houses or abandoned estates to lick up all the grime in the bath.
- **Size:** Unknown
- **Origin:** Nationwide
- **Most frequent place:** Baths

Danger	Immortality
Speed	Intelligence

Akaname, which appeared in an Edo period book called *Gazu Hyakki Yagyo*, has no written description whatsoever. There is only a picture of a thing with a single toe, sharp claws, and a protruding tongue. In a book called *Kokin hyaku monogatari kyomi*, also written in the Edo period, there is a record of a ghost called akaneburi which is said to appear in old bathhouses and dilapidated mansions. In the Showa and Heisei eras, Akaname was regarded as the same thing as Akaneburi. It is disgusting, but it may be like an automatic vacuum that cleans by itself.

Senpoku Kanpoku

A frog ghost that'll watch over the dead.

File.080

Rarity
★
★
★

Scariness

Characteristics: It has four legs and a human face. It watches over the dead.

Size: Size of a frog

Origin: Toyama Prefecture

Most frequent place: Houses

Danger	Immortality
Speed	Intelligence

Not many details are known, but apparently these Yokai have a human-like face, four legs, and look like toads. They appear in houses with dead people and watch over them. Many stories of Senpoku Kanpoku have been passed down in Toyama Prefecture.

It is said that after a person dies, Senpoku Kanpoku stay outside for a week to stand-guard, stay at the house for three weeks, and go to the grave after about four weeks.

Shizuka Mochi (Quiet Mochi)

It'll make sounds in the middle of the night, it's a sign of good fortune.

File.081

Rarity
☆ ☆ ☆

Scariness

- Characteristics: **It'll appear while making sounds of pounding mochi.**
- Size: **Unknown**
- Origin: **Tochigi Prefecture**
- Most frequent place: **Inside houses**

Danger	Immortality
Speed	Intelligence

Around 2:00 in the morning, you may hear the pounding sound of something approaching, and it may be good luck. Those who can hear the sound of an approaching Shizuka Mochi will be blessed with good luck. Conversely, those who hear the sound of the pounding moving away are told to turn away. It is a nice thing if it happens to you, but if you don't keep your ears open at 2:00 am, you are likely to miss your chance.

Okuri Ookami (Watcher Wolf)

It'll follow you until you make it home. If you keep calm, it'll be just fine.

File.082

Scariness

Rarity
⭐
⭐
⭐

- Characteristics: It'll follow people as they walk in the mountains at night and protect them from harm.
- Size: About the same as a wolf
- Origin: Mountains nationwide
- Most frequent place: Roads at night

Danger	Immortality
Speed	Intelligence

Okuri Ookami are said to follow people walking in the mountains and fields at night and give them a ride home. Stories are heard in various mountainous areas.

On the other hand, there is also a story that if a person falls down, it will bite him and he should never fall down. It seems that they are not good with fire. But basically, if you behave stoutly and do not harm them, they will protect you from other terrifying things. Their favorite food is salty. After your journey, you should thank them for their kindness and give them something like rice with salty red beans.

Kanedama

One day it suddenly drops out of nowhere and will fill that household with good luck.

File.083

Rarity
★
★
★

Scariness

MAX!

- Characteristics: **It is said Kanedama will bring good luck to the household it falls into.**
- Size: **Size of a meteorite**
- Origin: **Hyogo Prefecture**
- Most frequent place: **In front of houses**

| Danger | Immortality |
| Speed | Intelligence |

It is said that when Kanedama falls, the house will prosper. It is said to be in the Kanto area, Hyogo, and other areas. The color may be bright red, blue-white, or yellow.

It is said that a house in which Kanedama falls will prosper, and it is also acceptable to pick them up and place them in a tokonoma (alcove). However, it must be kept in its original state.

In an Edo period book titled *Konjaku gazu zoku hyakki*, a "kanrei" (gold spirit) similar to Kanedama appears. However, it is not known if it is the same thing as Kanedama. Since money is involved, it may be true.

Baku

It eats nightmares and replaces them with pleasant dreams.

File.084

Rarity
★
★
★

Scariness

MAX!

■ Characteristics: **It has the power to change nightmares to good dreams.**
■ Size: **Size of a bear**
■ Origin: **China and Japan**
■ Most frequent place: **Unknown**

Danger		Immortality			
Speed		Intelligence			

Baku is a spirit that eats nightmares and comes from China. According to a Chinese book titled *Honzo Tsunomoku*, Baku has the nose of an elephant, the eyes of a rhinoceros, the tail of an ox, the legs of a tiger, and its body resembles a bear. It seems to contain elements of various animals as much as Nue.

In Japan, it is said that when you have a nightmare, if you chant "I give last night's dream to Baku" three times, Baku will eat it. It is also said that Baku eats the nightmares and turns them into good dreams. There is also a custom to place a picture of a treasure ship with the word "baku" written on the sail under your pillow to have a good first dream.

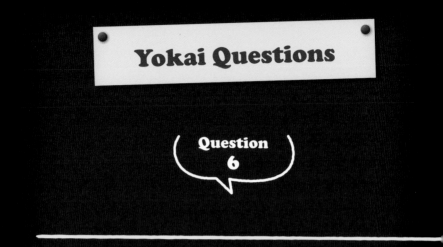

Yokai Questions

Question 6

When I try to do my homework,
I am immediately distracted by other
things and before I know it, time has
passed. I think it is probably because
of a Yokai. What should I do?

Don't blame everything on Yokai!
Why can't I do my homework? The answer is simple. It is because you are not doing it.

You may be thinking, "I won't die even if I don't do my homework." That is true. I used to think so too.

But homework is also a way to learn how to use your brain and train yourself to accomplish something.

It is important to keep at it, even if it is tedious or something you don't enjoy. The ability to get things done can be very useful when you are working. So don't look to Yokai for the solution. Look within yourself.

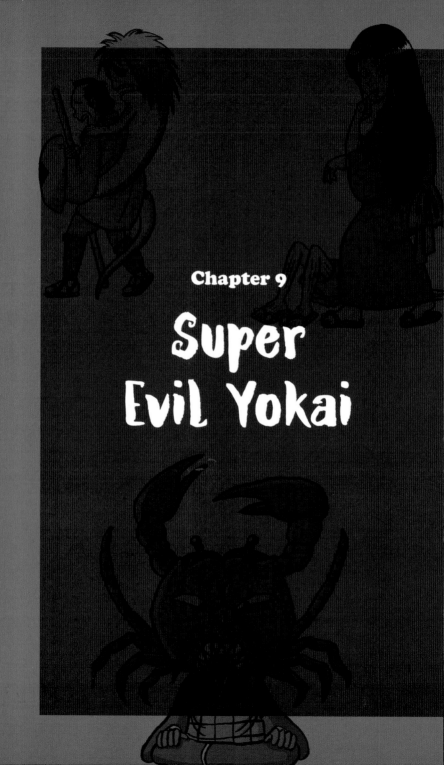

Chapter 9

Super Evil Yokai

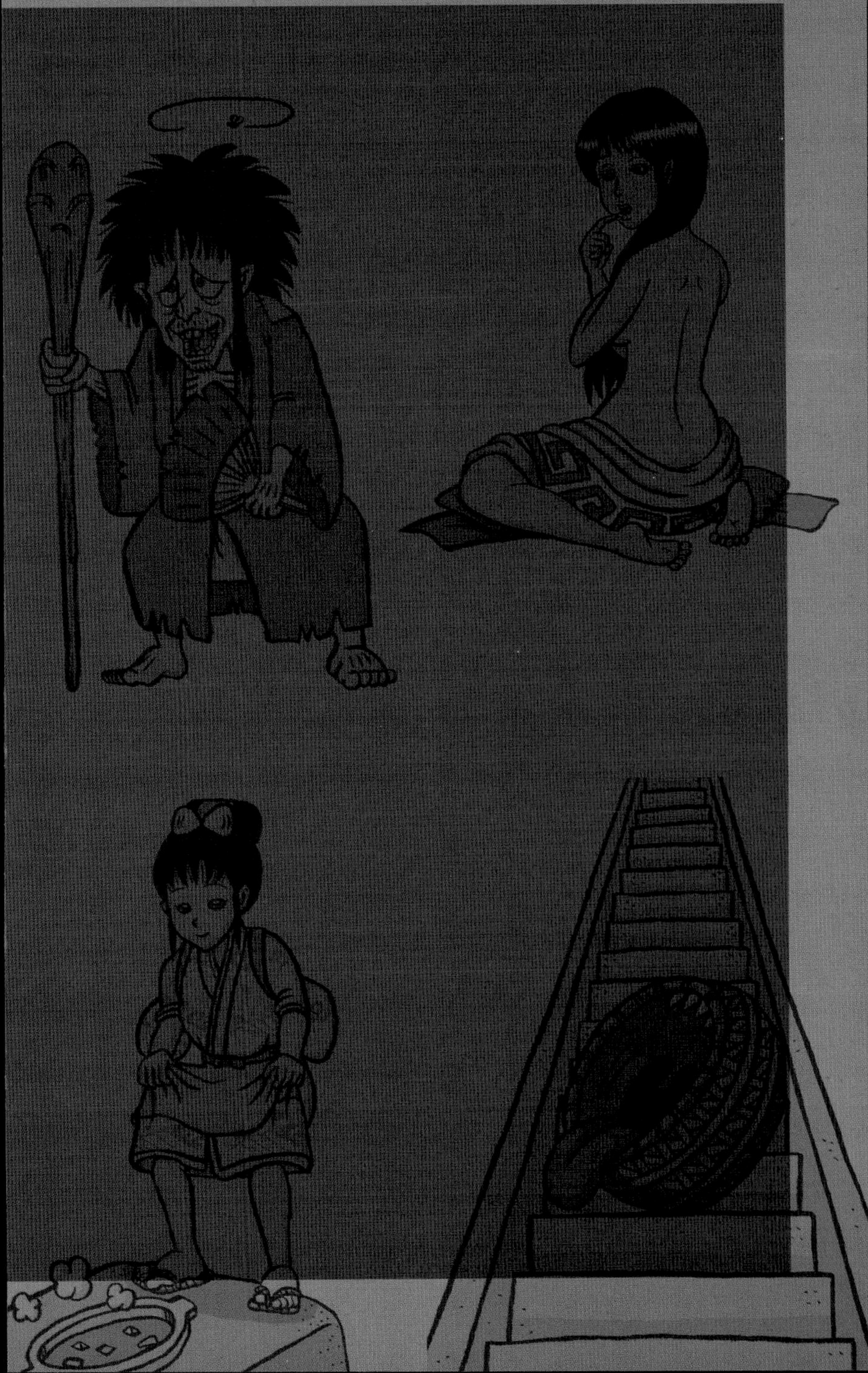

Kanibouzu (Crab Monk)

It'll kill you if you can't answer the question? A monster quizzing you at an abandoned temple.

File.085

Scariness

Rarity

★
★
★

MAX!

- Characteristics: It'll disguise itself as a monk, and appear in an empty temple to quiz those who stumble upon it.
- Size: About 10–13 ft. (3–4 m)
- Origin: Nationwide
- Most frequent place: Unattended temple

Danger

Immortality

Speed

Intelligence

As its name implies, Kanibozu is a crab Yokai. Several stories have been passed down, but most of them go like this. A traveling monk is staying at an empty temple when another monk appears and asks him a riddle. "What has eight legs and eight feet, moves sideways, and has eyes pointing toward the sky?" The traveling monk relized the truth and attacked the Yokai. He was lucky and survived, otherwise he would have been eaten.

This is SUPER Evil!

🔥 If you plan to stay overnight at a temple with no one around, be aware because it might appear

🔥 It'll quiz you... mostly things about himself

▶ Its true form is a crab

▶ It takes form of a very big monk

Interesting Fact

Be careful if you are given a riddle by a monk at a temple. It may be a Kanibouzu testing you.

Daru

Is it really the spirit of someone who starved to death? A Yokai that makes people hungry.

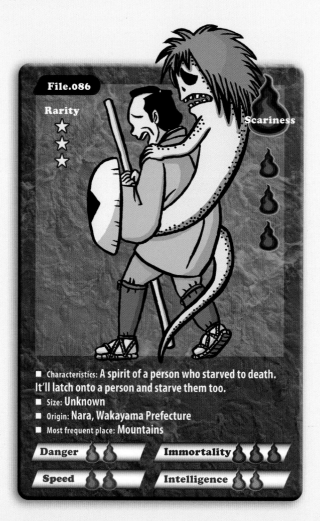

File.086

Rarity
★
★
★

Scariness

■ Characteristics: A spirit of a person who starved to death. It'll latch onto a person and starve them too.
■ Size: Unknown
■ Origin: Nara, Wakayama Prefecture
■ Most frequent place: Mountains

Danger		Immortality		

Speed		Intelligence		

It is said that when possessed by a Daru, a person becomes so hungry that he or she cannot move.

When you encounter a Daru, write the character for "米 rice" in the palm of your hand and lick it. The hunger will go away and your body will be set free. I also hear that it is a good idea to leave a bite of your lunch instead of eating the whole thing. If you get hungry easily, you might want to give it a try.

Pauchi Kamui

Kidnapping people and turning them into a completely different person? A Yokai that makes a big fuss and prefers to be naked.

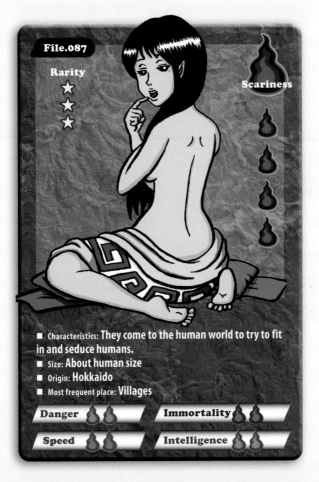

File.087

Rarity
★
★
★

Scariness

■ Characteristics: They come to the human world to try to fit in and seduce humans.
■ Size: About human size
■ Origin: Hokkaido
■ Most frequent place: Villages

Danger

Immortality

Speed

Intelligence

Pauchi Kamui is a form of taunting and is handed down in Ainu folklore. It seems that there are male and female Pauchi Kamui and both live their lives dancing around naked.

They usually live in a world separate from humans, but they occasionally appear in the human world and seduce people to join them. It is also said that humans cheat on each other because the Pauchi possesses them. But the worst thing may be when people cheat and feel no guilt and blame it all on Pauchi.

Hamaguri Nyobo (Clam Wife)

She may do something disgusting but she is an honest and admirable wife at heart.

File.088

Rarity
★
★
★

Scariness

- Characteristics: **She'll pee in home-cooked food and serve it to the man she loves.**
- Size: **About the same has a human**
- Origin: **Nara Prefecture** ■ Most frequent place: **Houses**

Danger			Immortality	

Speed		Intelligence			

One day a man was fishing when and he caught a large clam. After the clam had grown, a beautiful girl came to the man and asked him to marry her. The girl always cooked delicious dishes but she never showed him how she prepared the meals.

One day, the man was so curious about her secret that he peeked into the kitchen. To his surprise, he saw her peeing into the pot. Of course, this girl was a clam that the man had once saved.

Nikusui

A beautiful young woman in the mountains sucking people's flesh.

File.089

Rarity
★
★
★

Scariness

MAX!

- Characteristics: **It attacks people walking in the mountains by sucking up the life out of them.**
- Size: **About the same as a human**
- Origin: **Mie, Wakayama, Nara Prefecture**
- Most frequent place: **Mountains**

Danger

Immortality

Speed

Intelligence

Nikusui is a ghost that approaches people in the mountains and sucks their flesh. Stories are told in the mountains of Mie, Wakayama, and Nara. It is said that a beautiful woman of about 18 or 19 years of age will appear and ask you to lend her your fire so she can light her lantern, while giggling "Ho-ho-ho." It is a bit strange but not many people would refuse a request from a beautiful girl. If you agree to light her lantern, she will put out the fire and take a bite out of you.. It is said that the true identity of Nikusui is a skinny being that has been reduced to only bones and skin.

Bimbogami (Poor God)

The god who appears when we behave badly. It may be a god, but you don't want to meet this one.

File.090

Rarity
★

Scariness

MAX!

- **Characteristics:** It appears when you misbehave. He does not like clean houses.
- **Size:** Unknown
- **Origin:** Nationwide
- **Most frequent place:** Houses

Danger

Immortality

Speed

Intelligence

The god of poverty is an annoyance that puts people in a difficult situation. No one wants to meet him, but unfortunately, stories about Bimbogami have been passed down everywhere.

It is said that if you kneel while eating, tap your bowl, or whistle in the middle of the night, the god of poverty will come to you. Perhaps they like things that make noise.

Some say that what they don't like it when someone is burning wood or boiling red beans. There are also stories that if you worship them faithfully, they can become gods of good fortune.

Shinguri Makuri

A child that was placed in a basket and rolls down the stairs.

File.091

Rarity

★
★
★

Scariness

MAX!

- Characteristics: **A naughty child placed in a basket as discipline.**
- Size: **Size of a basket**
- Origin: **Nara Prefecture**
- Most frequent place: **Shrines**

| Danger | Immortality |
| Speed | Intelligence |

What a terrible ghost, to trap a child in it and roll down the stairs. In Yamazoe Village, Nara Prefecture, where the story is told, it is said that they roll children down from the top of a long flight of stairs. It would be better if they stop when the children is only dizzy, but it is said that they roll down the stairs of a shrine, which are so steep and long that they might injure the children. It seems that children who misbehave are put in the Shinguri Makuri. Grownups often try scare children by telling them, "Shinguri Makuri will come if you misbehave."

A Shrine Filled with Demon References

This is the only shrine with the name referencing "Kiou"

Inari Kiouji Jinja Shrine, a short walk from Higashi Shinjuku Station on the Tokyo Metro Fukutoshin Line, is located near a busy downtown area, yet the shrine has a serene atmosphere. The name "kiou," meaning

Inari Kiouji Jinja Shrine
Tokyo shinjiku kabukichou 2 chome 17-5
03(3200)2904

Demon King, may not be familiar to you but it seems that this is the only shrine in Japan with the name "kiou." Naotomo Okubo, the chief priest of the shrine, told us, "I think people have an image of demons being scary, but at the shrine we believe that demons have the same power as gods."

The water in the water basin is replaced daily

Onikata-water basin

It may not look as if the shrine is deeply connected to demons and the Suga family and as if it enshrines demons, but that is not the case. Kiou is said to refer to the three deities Tsukiyomi-no-mikoto, Omotono-no-mikoto, and Amatenashikio. In other words, Kiou is not equal to the demons themselves.

However, in reference to the name of Kiou, the priests chant "Fuku wa uchi, oni wa uchi" on Setsubun day, as demons are said to bring happiness. It is said that worshippers are also familiar with the shrine as a place where demons bestow clothes.

There is an interesting legend about a stone basin on the temple grounds. The demon is holding the stone basin above his head while stepping on four legs, and he has a scar on his shoulder.

It is said that this water basin stone stand was originally located in the garden of a certain Kagami. When he heard the sound of water every night, he cut the demon with his family's heirloom sword, and illness struck his family members. The scar on his shoulder was probably caused at that time. In 1833, the sword was donated to the shrine. It is said that pouring a washbasin of water over the sword's scar cures fevers and cries at night. Incidentally, the sword that was donated was stolen the year after the dedication and has never been found.

The cut on the stone that was done with a sword

Chapter 10

Super Stupid Yokai

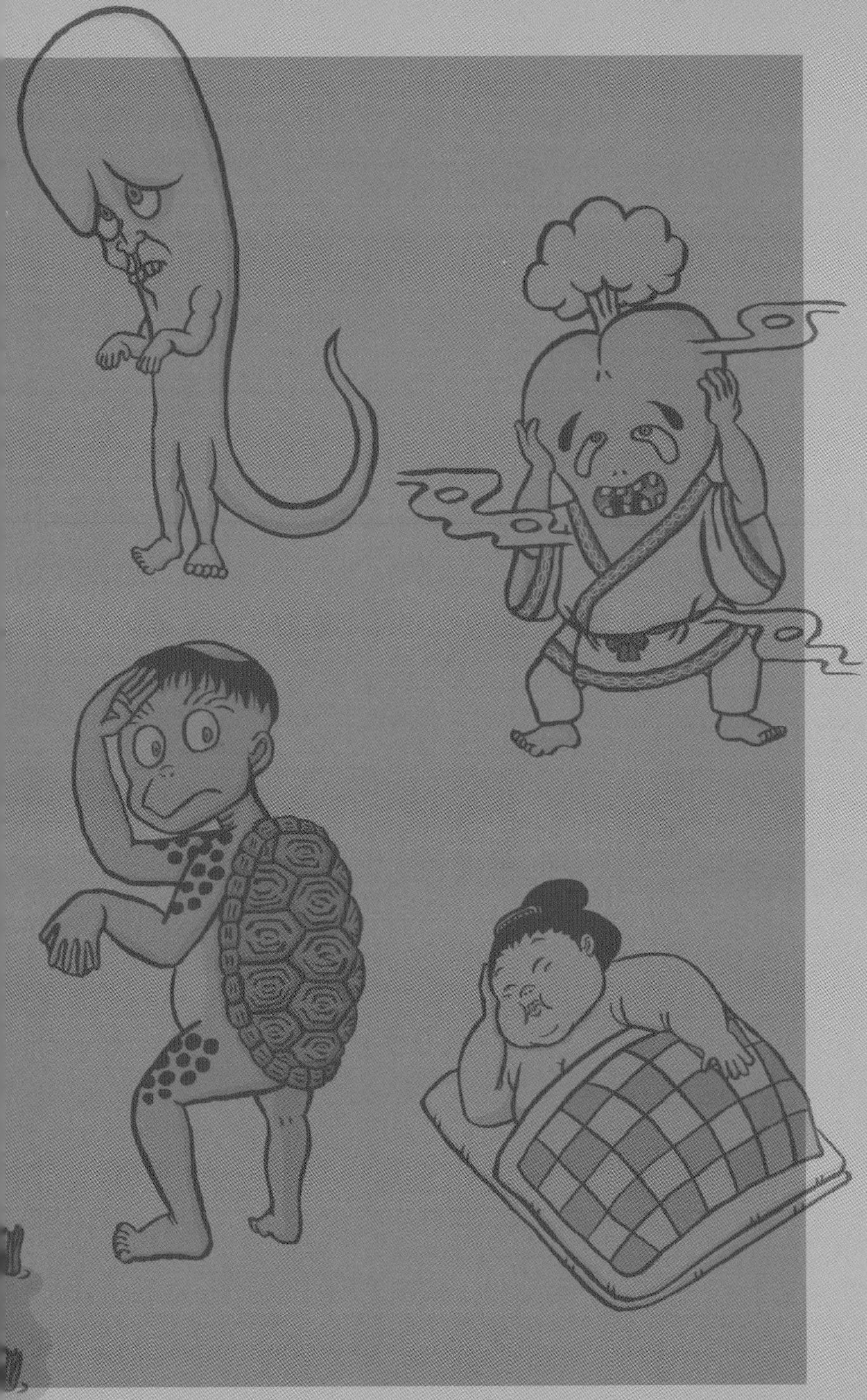

Biro-N

Is it the result of a failed transformation? It's so laughable.

File.092

Rarity
★
★
★

Scariness

MAX!

- Characteristics: Its body is like flubber, its tail is used to rub people's face.
- Size: Unknown
- Origin: Unknown
- Most frequent place: Unknown

Danger	?	Immortality	
Speed		Intelligence	

It is said that it is a ghost with a squishy body like a Konnyaku and that it strokes people's faces with its tail.

This "Biro-N" is said to be a spirit that tried to become a Buddha and failed. The spell chanted to become a Buddha was "BIRO-BIRO-BIRO-N."

Biro-N is also said to be another name for Nuributsu. It became well known when it was featured in children's Yokai illustrated books from the 1970s to the 1990s. It is said that they are not good with salt, and disappear when salt is poured on them. If you think about it, it's kind of like a slug.

This is SUPER Stupid!

💧 The transformation spell is "BIRO-BIRO-BIRO-N"

💧 It'll disappear if you pour salt on it

▶ Its body is squishy

▶ It rubs people with its tail

▶ It's a result of a failed transformation

💧 **Interesting Fact** 💧

Biro-N is a kind of Nuribotoke. It may be a Yokai that has been handed down only through the power of pictures, such as picture scrolls and Yokai illustrated books.

Tantankororin

It can produce delicious fruit from its butt? A persimmon Yokai that is too annoying.

File.093

Rarity
★
★
★

Scariness

MAX!

- ■ Characteristics: It's a big boy with a red face who will invite you to have a taste of its butt.
- ■ Size: Bigger than humans
- ■ Origin: Miyagi Prefecture
- ■ Most frequent place: Houses with persimmon trees

Danger	Immortality
Speed	Intelligence

This ghost is said to appear when persimmon fruits are left unripe.

It is said that when you are craving persimmons in the garden, a big man with a bright red face will come by and invite you to "have a taste of my butt." In the event you do what he says and lick it, you'll find that it tastes like a very sweet persimmon.

But really, what were you thinking? If you really want to eat a persimmon that much, is it necessary to go that far?

Dorotabo

A one-eyed black Yokai calling out, "Give me back my rice paddy!"

File.094

Rarity
★
★
★

Scariness

■ Characteristics: **It'll constantly beg for you to return the rice fields its descendants have neglected.**
■ Size: **Unknown**
■ Origin: **Northern Regions**
■ Most frequent place: **Rice fields**

Danger	Immortality
Speed	Intelligence

Dorotabo is a ghost that wants to have its rice paddies returned to it at any cost.

It appears in an Edo period book titled *Konjaku Hyakki Jikan Gen*. A man bought a rice paddy for his grandson. But after his death, his grandson neglected it. Then, night after night, a black thing with one eye came out and said, "Give me back my rice paddy!"

It seems that he was very attached to the rice paddy, but even if it was returned to him, there was nothing he could do about it in his ghostly state. So, let's just let him be.

Nebutori

A very large female ghost that snores loudly.

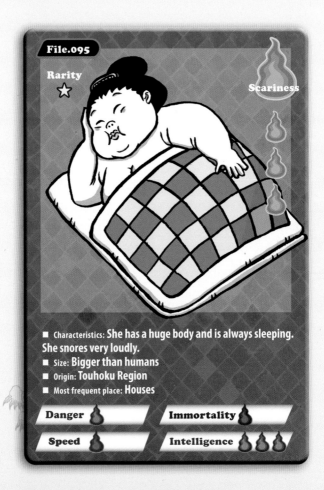

File.095

Rarity
☆

Scariness

■ Characteristics: **She has a huge body and is always sleeping. She snores very loudly.**
■ Size: **Bigger than humans**
■ Origin: **Touhoku Region**
■ Most frequent place: **Houses**

Danger		Immortality	
Speed		Intelligence	

Nebutori is said to be a ghost born to send a message to women.

It made an appearance in an Edo period book titled *Ehon Hyaku Monogatari* and is depicted as a giant girl. The description reads, "She makes a loud snore and is so noisy that she loses all her charm."

It is somewhat like listening to a complaint between married couples. But this kind of complaint is the same now as it was in the past. It is important to live one's life in one's own way without worrying only about what others think. However, if you stop caring so much, you may be haunted by Nebutori.

Usuoibaba

An old woman with a mortar on her back for some reason appears from the sea.

File.096

Rarity

Scariness

■ Characteristics: Carrying a Mortar on her back, she appears from the ocean once every 2–3 years.
■ Size: Unknown
■ Origin: Niigata Prefecture
■ Most frequent place: Oceans

Danger
Immortality
Speed
Intelligence

Usuoibaba is a ghost that appears from the bottom of the sea carrying a mortar on her back. The story has been passed down in Niigata Prefecture. Usuoibaba was first encountered by an angler on a day when he could not catch any fish.

Usuoibaba looks like an old lady and appears only once every two or three years and then disappears. She has a very frightening face, but I don't know why she is carrying a mortar on her back. If you leave her alone, she will disappear back to the bottom of the sea.

Tsukehimokozo

It'll constantly ask you to fix its untied clothes

File.097

Rarity
★
★
★

Scariness

- Characteristics: **It'll bother you all night asking you to help em fix its clothes.**
- Size: **Size of a child**
- Origin: **Nagano Prefecture**
- Most frequent sighting: **Azuki Togi Yashiki Mansion**

Danger

Speed

Immortality

Intelligence

Tsukehimokozu is a ghost wearing loose clothes and appears to walk around lost all night long. He is said to look like a child of about 7 to 8 years old, and appears around evening at a mansion called "Azuki Togi Yashiki" wearing clothes with untied strings.

If you encounter him, Tsukehimokozu will ask you to tie the strings back together, but for some reason, people will often find themselves walking around the house aimlessly. When dawn approaches, he will walk you home. So maybe he just wanted to take a walk with someone.

Tofukozo (Tofu Boy)

Weak Minded but good-natured? It carries a tray of tofu.

File.098

Rarity ☆☆☆

Scariness

MAX!

■ Characteristics:
It walks around while carrying a tray of tofu with an autumn leaf on top.
■ Size: Size of a child
■ Origin: Unknown
■ Most frequent sighting: Unknown

Danger		Immortality
Speed		Intelligence

Tofukozu is a ghost holding a tray with tofu on it. He is a good-natured ghost who does not do anything particularly violent. On the contrary, he is sometimes bullied by other Yokai. Some interpretations say that he carries tofu with a maple leaf symbol on it, which traditionally means that he is selling tofu.

Okkeruipe

He farts intensely, but when people fart on him, he's gone.

File.099

Rarity
★
★
★

Scariness

MAX!

- Characteristics: **It farts often and loudly. The best defense is to fart on him.**
- Size: **Unknown**
- Origin: **Hokkaido**
- Most frequent sighting: **Hearths**

Danger	Immortality
Speed	Intelligence

Okkeruipe is said to be an Ainu word for a ghost that farts intensely.

According to the story, he farts at the edge of a hearth. If it's just a small "toot," you may get the impression that it's a relatively gentle one. But the problem lies in the smell which is apparently unbearable.

If you fart back at the Okkeruipe, it will disappear. Unfortunately, if you can't seem to let out a fart, you can try saying "toot" and see if that works.

Kappa

It's strong and smart but how does it often get captured by humans?

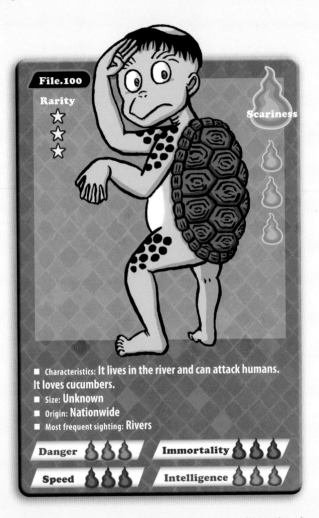

File.100

Rarity
★
★
★

Scariness

- Characteristics: It lives in the river and can attack humans. It loves cucumbers.
- Size: Unknown
- Origin: Nationwide
- Most frequent sighting: Rivers

Danger

Immortality

Speed

Intelligence

The Kappa is probably one of the most well-known Yokai. Stories of Kappa have been passed down throughout Japan as if they were real. Their nature and characteristics vary from region to region.

They are said to enjoy sumo wrestling as well as eating cucumbers and human butts. They can harm people, and there are horror stories about them. They are also said to be very strong and dependable, but they are sometimes captured. They are oddly goofy.

A Temple that Preserved a Kappa Hand

From Asakusa Station, you can walk to the famous town known as Kappabashi. It is a delightful street lined with various Kappa monuments, large and small. Entering Kappabashi from the main street, you will see Sogenji Temple. This temple is associated with Kappa.

There is a story about the area around the Kappa-bashi Bridge. In 1814, there was a man named Kawataro Kappa who invested his private funds in construction. During one construction, Kappa from the Sumida River, whose lives had once been saved by Kawataro, visited. It is said that when he saw those Kappa, his business mysteriously flourished. After his death, Kawataro was buried in Sogenji Temple, his family temple. Since then, the temple has been called "Kappa-dera," or Kappa Temple. The hall is decorated with a hanging scroll of the Kappa

Statue of "Kappa Kawataro." installed in the shopping arcade to commemorate the 90th anniversary of Kappabashi Dougu Street

Sogenji Temple
Tokyo Taitou Matsugaya 3-7-2
03(3841)2035

Sogenji Temple, also known as Kappa Temple

A hall called Kappa Daimyojin

deity, Hajifuku Kappa and paintings of Kappa drawn by various manga artists on the ceiling.

In addition, a mummy of a Kappa hand is kept in the exhibition space inside the hall. I was actually shown the hand, which was not stored in the hall at the time. It was found in a warehouse in Tokyo and brought to this temple because of its close connection to Kappa.

The temple's chief priest, Shusho Kuga, said, "There are many Kappa figures not only in the temple grounds but also in the shopping area, so visitors can go Kappa sightseeing."

Glass case inside the Kappa Daimyoujin where you can see a mummy of a Kappa hand.

Inside the Kappa Daimyoujin. You can see Kappa paintings by numerous artists on the ceiling.

Yokai List

Aburasumashi 59

Akago(Baby) 106

Akaname (Grime Licker) 138

Akaragashira 68

Ao Nyobo (Blue Lady) 107

Asaoke no Ke (Asaoke Hair) 40

Azukiarai (Red Bean Washer) 44

Baku 143

Betobeto-san (Mr. Sticky) 92

Bimbogami (Poor God) 154

Biro-n 160

Chin Chin Kobakama 48

Chinchirori 54

Chirami Kozo (Lurking Brat) 87

Daru 150

Dorotabo 163

Enenra 111

Gagoze 24

Ganborinyudo 120

Hainu (Winged Dog) 27

Hakutaku 134

Hamaguri Nyobo (Clam Wife) 152

Hitokusai (I-Smell-Human) 47

Hohonade (Cheek Rubber) 112

Ippon Datara 16

Iwanabouzu 126

Janjanbi 122

Kainade 82

Kamaitachi 113

Kamikiri (Haircutter) 136

Kanibouzu (Crab Monk) 148

Kappa 169

Karasu Ojisan (Uncle Crow) 57

Kasha (Fire Cart) 23

Kashambo 52

Kenedama 142

Keukegen 85

Kijimuna 99

Kincho-Tanuki 69

Kiyohime 22

Koromo-dako (Robe Octopus) 32

Kowai (Scary) 18

Kudan 46

Kune-Kune 31

Kusabira 94

Makuragaeshi (Pillow Swapper) 53

Mokurikokuri 124

Nakanekozou (Nakane Brat) 42

Nandobaba (Storage Room Granny) 86

Nebutori 164

Nekomata 26

Nikusui 153

Ningyo (Mermaid) 33

Notabozu 96
Nozuji 25
Nue 118
Nuppepo 83
Nurarihyon 56
Nurikabe (Painted Wall) 105
Okikumushi 123
Okkeruipe 168
Okuri Ookami (Watcher Wolf) 141
Oshiroi-Baba (Powder Granny) 108
Otekurebaba (Piggy-Back-Ride-Me Granny) 84
Otoroshi 49
Pauchi Kamui 151
Peroritaro (Licky Boy) 55
San no Maru-Gaeru (Castle Outskirt Frogs) 129
Satori 29
Sennenmogura (Thousand-Year-Old-Mole) 51
Senpoku Kanpoku 139
Shinguri Makuri 155
Shiri-Haguri 50
Shizuka Mochi (Quiet Mochi) 140
Shunobon 20
Shutendoji 70

Sodehikikozou (Sleeve Tugging Brat) 98
Soroban Bozu (Abacus Boy) 127
Sumitsuke (Painter) 104
Sunekosuri 97
Tamamonomae 72
Tantankororin 162
Tatarimokke 125
Tenaga-Ashinaga (Long-Limbed Giants) 78
Tengu 73
Tenome (Eye Hands) 80
Tofukozo (Tofu Boy) 167
Tomokazuki 30
Tsuchigumo 71
Tsukehimokozo 166
Ubume 128
Ushioni (Ox Demon) 66
Usuoibaba 165
Uwan 38
Yagyou-San (Mr. Nightwalker) 45
Yamamba 28
Yamatano-Orochi 64
Yanari 109
Yosuzume (Night Sparrow) 110
Zashikiwarashi 58

Final Words

Sometimes reading a book can give you a strange feeling. I believe that sometimes it can affect you for the rest of your life. I have always been a person who reads books whenever I have time. Among them, I am especially fond of mysterious stories with ghosts. When I had just entered high school, my teacher asked me to think about my career path. I had just read Akiko Baba's *Oni no Kenkyu* (*The Study of Demons*), and I told my teacher that I wanted to study demons at university. That's how I found my way to writing this book.

I am sure that you, too, are interested in Yokai to one degree or another. As a writer, I would be more than happy if, after reading this book, you now have a greater appreciation for Yokai. However, if you get too absorbed in this book, you may end up becoming infatuated with Yokai, like me. Welcome to my world. Let's go and discover Yokai together!

Lastly, I would like to thank the Tatsumi publishing team for inviting me to write *Nara Yokai Shinbun* (*Nara Yokai Newspaper*), which I have been writing by myself in a corner of Nara. I would also like to thank Shigeo for the wonderful illustrations in this book. Shigeo gave me a lot of ideas for the book, even from the earliest stage of deciding which Yokai to include. I am sure it must have been very difficult for you to support me as I was out of the loop here and there. Thank you all for your hard work.

I believe that Yokai have the power to make people happy. I hope that those who picked up this book will also be infected with this happy germ.

—Masami Kinoshita

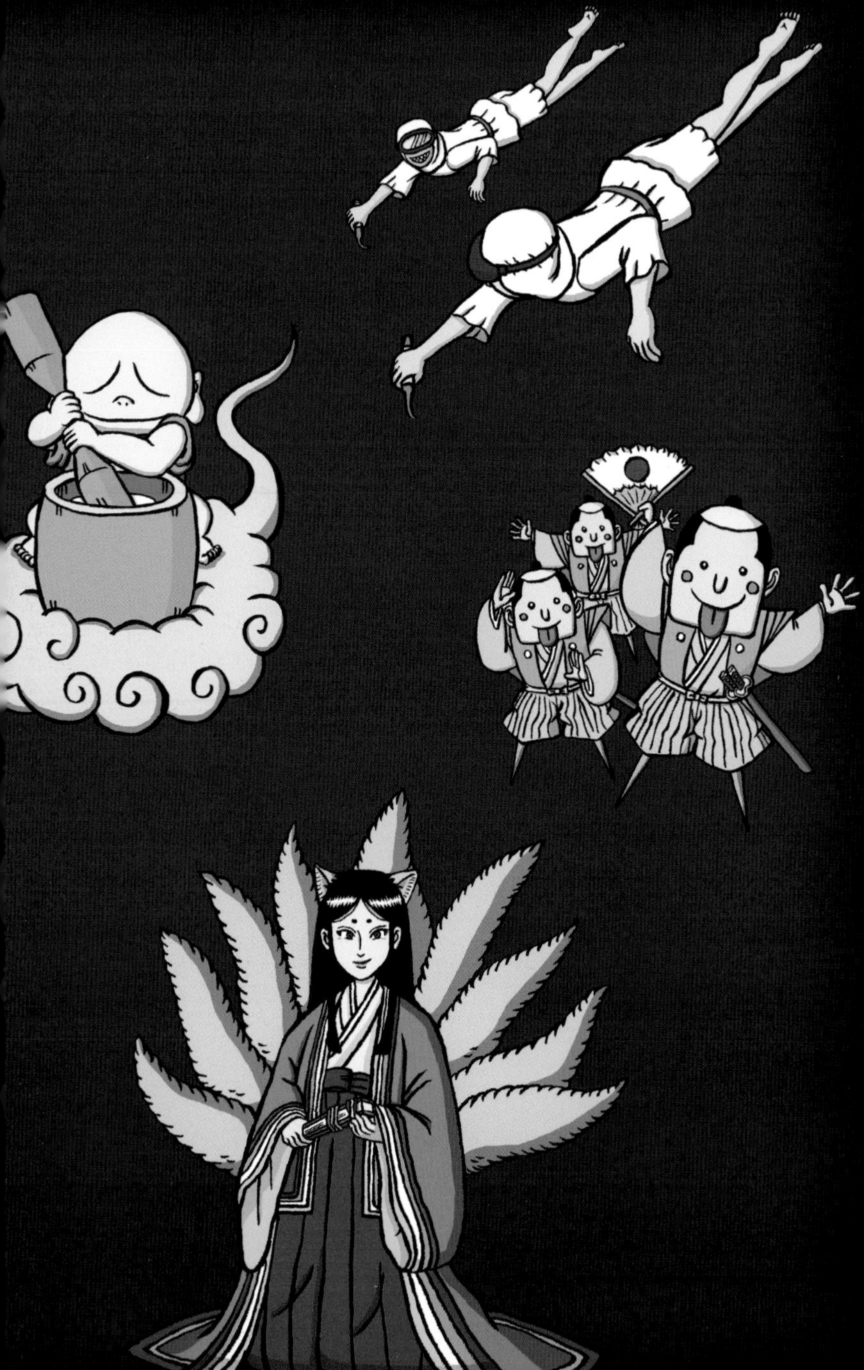

Published by Tuttle Publishing, an imprint of Periplus Editions (HK) Ltd.

www.tuttlepublishing.com

ISBN: 978-4-8053-1728-0

English Translation © 2023 Periplus Editions (HK) Ltd.

SUGOIZE! NIPPON YOKAI BIKKURI ZUKAN
Copyright © MASAKI KINOSHITA,
TATSUMI PUBLISHING CO., LTD.2019
All rights reserved.
English translation rights arranged with
TATSUMI PUBLISHING CO., LTD. through
Japan UNI Agency, Inc., Tokyo

Staff (Original Japanese edition)
Illustrator Hidemitsu Shigroka
Designer Seika Omi (Plan Link)
Editor Ando San (Goes)
Planning manager Yuji Hirose

Distributed by
North America, Latin America & Europe
Tuttle Publishing
364 Innovation Drive
North Clarendon, VT 05759-9436 U.S.A.
Tel: 1 (802) 773-8930; Fax: 1 (802) 773-6993
info@tuttlepublishing.com
www.tuttlepublishing.com

Japan
Tuttle Publishing
Yaekari Building, 3rd Floor
5-4-12 Osaki
Shinagawa-ku
Tokyo 141-0032
Tel: (81) 3 5437-0171; Fax: (81) 3 5437-0755
sales@tuttle.co.jp
www.tuttle.co.jp

Asia Pacific
Berkeley Books Pte. Ltd.
3 Kallang Sector #04-01
Singapore 349278
Tel: (65) 6741-2178; Fax: (65) 6741-2179
inquiries@periplus.com.sg
www.tuttlepublishing.com

26 25 24 23   8 7 6 5 4 3 2 1
Printed in Malaysia   2307VP